W9-BAU-232

EIGHTEEN
WINTERS

ALSO BY JOANNE DEMAIO

The Winter Novels
Snowflakes and Coffee Cakes
Snow Deer and Cocoa Cheer
Cardinal Cabin
First Flurries
Eighteen Winters
Winter House
—And More Winter Novels—

The Seaside Saga
Blue Jeans and Coffee Beans
The Denim Blue Sea
Beach Blues
Beach Breeze
The Beach Inn
Beach Bliss
Castaway Cottage
Night Beach
Little Beach Bungalow
Every Summer
Salt Air Secrets
Stony Point Summer
The Beachgoers
Shore Road
—And More Seaside Saga Books—

Beach Cottage Series
The Beach Cottage
Back to the Beach Cottage

Summer Standalone Novels
True Blend
Whole Latte Life

eighteen
winters

A NOVEL

JOANNE DEMAIO

This is a work of fiction. Names, characters, places, and incidents are either the product of the author's imagination or are used fictitiously. Any resemblance to actual persons, living or dead, events, or locales is entirely coincidental.

No part of this book may be reproduced, or stored in a retrieval system, or transmitted in any form or by any means, electronic, mechanical, photocopying, recording, or otherwise, now known or hereinafter invented, without express written permission of the copyright owner.

Copyright © 2019 Joanne DeMaio
All rights reserved.

ISBN: 9781079270457

Joannedemaio.com

*To the card-sending couple
who inspired this special story*

With gratitude.

one

The First Winter

HOME. HARRY DANE CAN'T WAIT to get ther
again. But this time, it won't be the same—so the driv
home feels different.

Taking the turnoff into the town of Addison, he le
up on the gas. At long last, he cruises the familiar stre
of his Connecticut hometown. The country roads
lined with saltbox colonials and New England Cape Co
Some have garland strung around lampposts and acr
white picket fences. He sees a birch-log deer on a po
stoop. Balsam wreaths hang on doors. The sk
December blue; the air, crisp. All is achingly familiar
drives past the local coffee shop, the town green, Co
Hardware—its side lot strung with light bulbs over
display of fresh-cut Christmas trees for sale.

But when Harry turns and drives along Bro
Road, passing English Tudors and farmhouses se
on front lawns, that hopeful going-home feeling cl

Rounding a curve, he sees the covered bridge up ahead. That's when his anticipation fades. His excitement lessens. Because for the first time ever, he's going home to a *different* house—one he's never been inside before. The family's the same, as is the town. But not long after Harry left a few months ago, his parents sold their old colonial and moved to a smaller place. So the home he remembers is now gone.

Moments later, the car tires thump across the wooden planks of the covered bridge. While driving beneath the bridge's dark timbers, it feels like Harry's passing through some sort of time machine. Historic Olde Addison is on the other side. His family's new home is, too—set somewhere among historic ship captains' houses on wide, tree-lined streets. Streets leading to the silver expanse of the cove.

Harry eventually turns onto Birch Lane, passing a small Victorian, a shingled ranch, a Garrison colonial. He glances at the house numbers until the right one comes into view. After pulling into the driveway, he squints through the windshield to the olive-green Craftsman bungalow. It's clapboard sided, with a shingled second-story front dormer and a large stone chimney. From the pitched roof, an overhang extends over the wide front porch.

So *this* is home now, though it doesn't feel like it.

Not until the front door opens and Harry's father stands there. He's wearing a burgundy cardigan sweater over his flannel shirt and corduroy pants. His hand shields his eyes while he bends and peers out to the driveway.

As Harry gets out of the car, his father hurries down the few porch steps and along the stone walkway. "Harry!" he calls out as he nears. "Harry, good to have

2

you home again!" Right when Harry sets down his duffel, his father does it. He hugs him, warmly clapping his back.

"Hey, Pop," Harry says. "Really missed you."

"Me, too." His father steps back, smiling.

After lifting his duffel with one hand, Harry loops his other arm across his father's shoulders. Together, they walk side by side toward the front porch.

⌒◯

An hour and a double-decker ham-and-cheese sandwich later, Harry is up to date on his family's new home. During several autumn tag sales, his parents had downsized so that only the best of the best—the furniture and accessories with the fondest memories—remained. Finally, only four days ago, the moving truck brought all that remaining furniture crosstown to their smaller Craftsman bungalow. Over lunch now at the farm table—which made the cut *and* the move—Harry learns that one day after the closing on this house, a second real estate closing happened.

"So you *really* bought the store?" Harry asks as he rinses his plate at the sink, then returns to the table.

"We did." His mother, Linda, wipes crumbs off the counter. "Bought the building, the inventory, the display racks. All of it."

"Just like we told you, son," his father adds. "Used the profit from the sale of that big house to buy the Addison General Store." Sitting in a chair beside Harry, he clasps his arm. "It seemed like the right time. Your sister will be graduating from college in the spring, and you're halfway through your freshman year in Boston now. Your mom and I are practically empty nesters, ready for a change."

"I get it. It makes perfect sense, Pop. You've been managing that store for the past ten years and know it inside out," Harry admits. "But you don't think it'll be too much, running the whole show there?"

"Not at all. It's what I've been *wanting* to do all those ten years."

"Norm," Harry's mother says from the refrigerator, where she's returning the mayonnaise to a shelf. "Now that we've had lunch, why don't you give Harry the grand tour of the house?"

For the next half hour, Harry walks through his family's Craftsman bungalow. Wide crown molding lines each gold-painted room. White wainscoting reaches halfway up the dining room walls. In the living room, built-in dark wood shelves flank either side of the stone fireplace. Everywhere he looks—from the barnwood flooring to the rough-hewn mantel—Harry notices the impressive architecture of the home.

"And this here," his father says when he turns into a room off the kitchen, "is *your* room, Harry."

"*My* room? But I live away, Pop. I'll be on campus most of the time."

"And when you're not at college, you have a space here to rest your head."

"But it's a waste of space. You can put it to better use," Harry insists as he walks across the room, where his mother already deposited his duffel and overnight bag on the bed.

"No, no. We'll always have a room for you, Harry," she says from the doorway now.

Harry looks back at her. "What about an office, Ma? Since you're running the general store with lots of ledgers and paperwork to manage, you'll need a home office. You can just put a pull-out couch in it for when I'm here."

"We have an office at the store," his father tells him. "We're still getting settled in there, too. I'm making some changes, sprucing things up. Reviewing some vendor samples."

"Again? Must be because we invited submissions in our newspaper ad," Linda says. "What samples came in?"

"Candies, farm-fresh jams, homemade candles folks want us to carry." Norm turns back to Harry. "So listen, son. Think you'll be able to put in a few hours' work at the store on your break? It'd be a big help. And we'd pay you, of course."

When Harry agrees, they spend the next hour ironing out a work schedule while unrolling a braided rug across the living room floor, and while rearranging the sofa and coffee table there. Harry helps his father unpack boxes of framed photos and pewter pitchers and brass candlesticks. With that done, his father leaves to pick up a Christmas tree from the hardware store.

"House is taking shape, Ma. Looking more and more like home," Harry says while folding an empty moving carton. "What do you want me to do now?"

"Why don't you get the mail? I heard the truck go by a little while ago."

After returning minutes later with a handful of envelopes, Harry closes the front door behind him. "You got a few Christmas cards, Ma," he calls out.

"Go ahead and open them," Linda calls back from the kitchen.

So he does. Harry settles in a tufted armchair beside the stone fireplace and looks around at this new living room, where new memories will be made. Where the tree will be put up and decorated tomorrow, in time for the holiday. Where lights on its boughs will glow in the dusky evenings. Where presents wrapped with care will be placed. Where morning sunbeams will fall through paned windows onto the dark wood floors.

But for now, he tears open the envelopes and pulls out one Christmas card, then another. He looks at the festive, snowy scenes and reads the sentiments inside: one from an aunt and uncle, another from a family friend in their old apple-orchard neighborhood.

The name on the third card, though, isn't familiar. It's signed from someone named Sadie. So he flips the card closed and looks at the image on the front. Two crisscrossed candy canes are wrapped with a fancy red bow. When he opens the card again, he reads the personal message penned beneath the verse.

Merry Christmas, Lorrie. Miss you.

From,
Sadie

Lorrie? Harry picks up the envelope and brings it, along with the card, to the kitchen. "Do you know these people?" he asks his mother there.

She looks back from where she's stacking coffee cups

in a painted cabinet. "What people?"

"Lorrie and Allan. Their names are on the envelope, but it's addressed to *this* house."

"Oh, yes!" His mother turns and takes the envelope from him. "They lived here for many years, Lorrie and Allan. They're the folks we bought the house from." She opens the card and reads the note inside. "That's sweet," she softly says. "But this … *Sadie*. Well, she must not realize that Lorrie and Allan have moved away." His mother gives him the envelope again. "Put it in the drawer, would you, Harry? In that end table in the living room, where it'll be safe and out of the way while we move in. Hate to lose it in all this clutter."

"You don't want me to just toss it?" Harry asks as he turns back toward the living room.

"What? No. I'll drop that—Sadie, is it?"

"Yes, Sadie." From the kitchen doorway, Harry glances at the envelope's return address. "Sadie Welles."

His mother lifts another mug to the cabinet shelf and says over her shoulder, "I'll drop poor Sadie a line after the holidays. To let her know Lorrie and Allan don't live here anymore."

two

The Second Winter

HARRY STANDS ON MAIN STREET in front of the general store. The store occupies the inside of an old two-story farmhouse. Its dark brown wood-planked siding and white-trimmed windows give the building a rustic feel. An *Open* sign hangs on the entrance door, and beside it, pinecones are nestled in a big balsam wreath. Harry's gaze moves up to the brand-new store sign above the porch.

"A little to the left, Norm." Harry's mother motions for his father to shift over the propped-up sign, all while she holds her movie camera to her eye. "Another inch," she calls up to him on his ladder.

From where Harry stands on the sidewalk, he reads the words painted on the long rectangular piece of wood. "*Dane's General Store*," he whispers. It feels good saying that. Feels good acknowledging his father's dream-come-true. The new store sign is a gift from Harry's mother this second Christmas of their store ownership. Harry reads the smaller words painted beneath the store name. *Storekeeper: Norman Dane*. And on each end of the long sign, there's a short list of the store's main inventory. *Home Goods. Postcards. Gifts*, on one side. And on the right side, *Coffee. Sundries. Conversation*. He likes that, Harry decides with a nod. Conversation. Squinting up at the words, at *Dane's General Store*, he returns to his ladder leaning against the storefront. There, he climbs to the top rung to help his father secure the sign. The two of them give a wave down to Linda's movie camera before she heads back inside the store.

"Glad you'll be working here again on your winter break," his father says then while extending his measuring tape across the rooftop toward Harry.

"Looking forward to it, Pop. Can't believe you've owned the place for a year now." From his ladder, Harry carefully measures the distance from the edge of the sign to the white trim on the peaked second level. "I miss anything exciting this fall, while I was away?"

"Well," Norm says, marking the wood siding with a thick pencil point. "We did the scarecrow thing, for the town competition. Made ours a farmer with overalls, his straw arms tilling a garden off to the side there," he says, nodding to the yard below. "You know, a tip of the hat to the original owners of this old farmhouse, before it became a store."

"You get the trophy?"

"Not this year, son. But I'll try again next fall. Someday, I'd love to win a trophy for the store." Norm tucks his pencil behind his ear and leans back from his ladder perch. "We need my level, Harry. To make sure the sign's straight. Would you get it for me?"

"Where is it?" Harry asks, already descending his own ladder on the far side of the sign. "Inside?"

"No. At home, in the garage. The big level, hanging on the wall."

Harry stops mid-rung. "Do we really need it? I've got a good eye," he says, tipping his head and gauging the sign's placement.

"Harry." His father descends, one careful step after the other, to the sidewalk. "If you're doing a job, you do it right. Especially when it involves the family name."

"Okay, Pop. For you, I'll get the level. You go help Mom inside. Got some customers shopping in there."

❦

Harry takes the store's delivery van and drives the country roads home. The wind is blowing today, fluttering balsam garlands and velvet wreath ribbons. Though it hasn't snowed yet this December, it feels like those falling white flakes are imminent.

Turning onto Birch Lane and seeing the Craftsman bungalow down the street, Harry realizes something. And what it is, is this: Finally, this second Christmas here, that olive-green bungalow with tapered porch columns; with paned windows looking out of a shingled loft dormer; with a twinkling tree in the living room? It's feeling more and more like home.

When he pulls into the driveway, the mail truck is approaching. So Harry gets out and walks over.

"Hey there, Harry," the mailman, Pete Davis, says as

he stops at the curb. "You home from college?"

"Winter break. Going back in January."

"What are you now, a junior?"

"No. I'm in my second year. A business major."

"Good for you, Harry."

"Helping my folks at the store when I'm home, too."

"Nice way to put your education to use. In the family business," Pete says as he hands Harry a bundle of envelopes. "Nothing like working with family, I can vouch for that. My son's a mailman, too. Wes. Just started. Didn't you go to high school with him?"

"I did. Wes was a couple of years ahead of me."

"Thought so. And now he works with me. It's always nice to meet up on our routes, or for lunch."

Harry salutes Pete, then turns to go inside. "Say hi to Wes for me, would you?" Harry calls back before climbing the porch steps and unlocking the front door. Once inside, he thumbs through the mail. The electric bill and department store flyer he sets on the kitchen counter. But the handful of Christmas cards he opens, looking at a photograph of his cousins that his aunt sent along. The next two cards carry holiday greetings from nearby neighbors, and … wait. This last envelope's oddly familiar. He reads the message penned beneath the card's verse.

Happy Holidays, Lorrie! I started driver's ed this fall. Maybe someday I can drive to Addison, and we'll have lemonade on your porch swing again.

xoxo,
Sadie

"Sadie, Sadie," Harry quietly says as he looks at the front of the card. On it, two red cardinals are perched on a wooden fence post. He looks at the envelope again and sees that Sadie addressed it to the same people as last year's card: Lorrie and Allan, at *this* house. Harry remembers his mother saying she'd send Sadie a note, to let her know that the couple had moved. So he puts the card back in the envelope and drops it in the same living room end table drawer—the one still holding last year's candy cane card.

By the time Harry gets back to the general store with the level, his father is pacing outside near the ladders. So Harry turns up his jacket collar against that cold wind before they both climb up to the rooftop again. As Harry extends the level across the top of the new sign, he notices something down below. There's an opening in the latticework beneath the store's porch area. From where he stands on the top ladder rung, it looks like a piece of that lattice has been pushed back, over on the side of the porch.

After first remeasuring the porch rooftop to be sure that the long wooden sign is mounted straight, Harry climbs down his ladder. His father gives him a thumbs-up as he descends, too, then folds up the ladders.

But all the while, that damaged lattice is bothering Harry. Any animal might get behind it, to the crawlspace beneath the porch. Could do serious damage, too, if it's a woodchuck, or raccoon, maybe. On the cold ground,

Harry gets down on his knees and bends low, moving closer when a quiet sound comes. He squints into the shadows under the wooden floorboards, then goes inside the store for a flashlight.

"What've you got there?" his father asks after returning the two ladders to the storage barn behind the store.

"Hey, Pop." Harry, back on his knees outside, motions to the hole in the lattice. "Check this out."

∽

And so it is the year of the kittens. A litter of five, along with their mother, were nestled in dried leaves beneath the porch. Harry's mother had the local vet examine each furry feline, after which she hung a *Found* poster in the general store's front window.

But … nothing.

No one claimed ownership of the five kittens and one cat. So it ends up being the year of a unique item for sale at Dane's General Store. A fun item, too, as Harry and his father manage to get all the kittens inside in a basket lined with soft rags. They keep the basket in a large cage on loan from the veterinarian's office. But the cage door is never closed as the fluffy kittens scamper and somersault and sashay across the checkerboard floor and on top of counters at Dane's General Store.

Gradually, as the days close in on the holiday, the kittens dwindle, though. One by one. A mother with two small children wraps the tiniest kitten in a scarf; a young couple tucks the most plaintive in a cloth bag; an older gentleman settles the mama cat in a small carton. The store grows quiet again as each remaining kitten is brought home to one family or another.

But still, on Christmas Eve, Harry is glad that there were smiles all around that one week, the year the general store had a happy sign in the front window: *Kittens for Christmas.*

three

The Third Winter

HARRY SHOULD'VE KNOWN.

From the moment he lifted the store's delivery van key off the wall hook, he should've known.

When he told the guys, "Quick! Get in, get in!" while parked in each of their driveways, he should've known.

The entire time he gunned it up the highway north in that van—Greg Davis sitting in the front passenger seat, and Frank Lombardo, Nate Carbone and Steve Pine stowed in the cargo area with their snowboards and gear—it was obvious.

The whole ride was totally illegal. Totally wrong. Harry and his old high school buddies were home from college on winter break. And they were *breaking* every rule in the book: driving a stolen vehicle; the friends in the back of the van not seatbelt-buckled; speeding on the highway. But they couldn't resist. Frank's college roommate works at a nearby ski area and dangled free lift tickets and free equipment rentals in front of their empty wallets. Not to mention, it was a Friday night, with the hours begging to be filled.

Then Steve's clunker car wouldn't start and all phones rang Harry.

Harry, with access to a delivery van once his father closed up the general store.

Harry, who waited in the shadows until his father drove his car out of the parking lot and headed home. Then, and only then, did Harry sneak in the store's rear entrance—just enough to reach his arm in the doorway and snag that van key.

Harry, who wavered even while driving on the highway. His father would kill him if he discovered the missing van. But the others persuaded him, regardless.

Don't worry, guy. We'll be back by midnight.
One o'clock, tops.
Your old man won't even know the difference.
We'll pitch in and gas up the tank, too.

Though the whole night was too risky, his friends convinced him it would be worth it. They'd have a good time, none the worse for wear.

Back it up right there, Harry thinks now from a hospital emergency room. That's where the night stops—*none the worse for wear.* Because he actually *became* worse for wear when he fumbled and hopped off the ski lift all wrong. Yes, the good times came to a sudden halt when he landed awkwardly, catching himself before crashing into the packed snow. Catching himself with his outstretched left arm that snapped funny. His arm from which a sudden lump swelled.

A lump that the staff at the ski area insisted needed immediate medical attention, so Nate and the guys drove Harry to the local hospital.

A hospital where Harry and his friends spend hours in the packed waiting room among twisted ankles, coughs, ski bruises and bumps, and fevers. Harry's friends pace. They watch the mounted TV. They joke. They quiet as the minutes tick into the early morning hours.

"Nate," Harry finally says from the chair where he's resting his injured arm. "Do me a favor."

"Sure, Harry." Nate crosses the room and sits beside him. "Name it."

"My father will be really upset if he finds the store's delivery van missing." Harry reaches into his jeans pocket and gives Nate the key again. "You guys take off."

"What?" Frank asks from where he stands near a wall of windows overlooking the parking lot. His ski cap is still on, and he fidgets with heavy snow gloves.

"Go home," Harry insists. "Get the van back to the general store. Then one of you can come and pick me up with your own car. Or your parents' car. Whatever."

"I'll stay here with you," Greg tells him. "Keep you company."

With the plan in place, the others walk out the emergency room door and leave. Harry breathes some sort of sigh of relief, hoping beyond hope Nate can pull it off. If anyone can, it's Nate Carbone—with his daredevil attitude, with his way of pushing the limits. He'd be the one to get that van safely back to Addison without much of a sweat.

At least, until a siren and flashing lights pull up close to the van's rear bumper.

Greg gets *that* call on his cell phone an hour later.

"Cops pulled us over!" Frank manages in a hushed voice. "Two cruisers. They have Nate outside. Mentioned something about grand theft. We're screwed, man."

No, Harry thinks when Greg tells him what happened. *I'm screwed*. No lawbook thrown at Nate can match the weight of what's surely coming Harry's way—his father's angry reaction.

"Shoot!" Harry says as he sits, now with a full cast on his lower left arm. "Busted. And they were supposed to come back and pick us up."

"Maybe my father will come get us," Greg tells him.

"Seriously? That'd be awesome, because my dad'll be working at the store." Harry glances out the waiting room windows. "After he calms down, he will be anyway. You really think Pete will drive up here?"

"He won't like it, but I'll just call him and explain what happened," Greg tells him. "I'll try to put a good spin on it."

Which Greg does. He calls his father, Pete Davis. Pete, the mailman who actually lives on Birch Lane a few doors down from Harry and his family.

Pete, who agrees to take care of things. What he conveniently left out is that *he* wouldn't be the one driving the highway north to pick up Greg and Harry.

Norm would, Harry realizes a couple of hours later. Still sitting in the waiting room midmorning, Harry's heart drops. Oh, and there's no recovering it, either. Not when he sees his father push through the glass entrance doors to the hospital emergency room.

✑

Whoever said that silence is golden wasn't sitting in the car with Harry and his father. Silence is golden? It's more like torture. More like it's thick as pea soup. More like you could slice it with a knife, it's so laden with tension. But even then, Harry's not sure which is worse: the silence, or his father's quiet words that finally break it twenty minutes later.

"You put the Dane name to shame, Harry, stealing a vehicle like that."

"Pop." Harry shifts in the front seat of his father's car. "I just made a mistake. But we didn't mean any harm."

"Mistake? You're lucky you only broke a wrist. What if you'd been in a car accident with all those guys stashed in the store van? Your friends would've been seriously hurt. You're a college junior already, and should know better."

"All right. All right. I get it. I'm sorry."

"Mr. Dane," Greg says from the backseat. "We kind of pressured Harry. Steve's car broke down and we pushed Harry to take the van, which would fit all of us *and* our snowboards."

"Gregory," Norm says with a glance in the rearview mirror. "Your father's very disappointed in you especially. With your plans to go on to medical school and behaving this way? For what?" he asks Greg. "To fly down a mountain? A lot of good it all did."

"What about Nate?" Harry eventually asks. "Is he at the police station?"

"No. He's home," Harry's father says as he finally drives the car through Addison's covered bridge and onto Birch Lane. He pulls up in front of the Davis' Victorian.

19

"Once I vouched for Nate's story, the charges were dropped. But the trouble's not," he adds as Greg gets out and heads to his house. Norm doesn't leave there until he sees Greg's father, Pete, open the front door and wave to him.

Silently, then, Norm drives with Harry further down the block to their own house. Once he pulls in the driveway, he just sits in the idling car. A few more strained moments pass as Harry looks out at the Craftsman bungalow all decked out for the holidays. Candles are in the windows; a balsam wreath hangs on the planked front door; garland wraps around the lamppost. All of it pales now, beside the reality of Harry's one foolhardy decision.

Without looking over at Harry in the passenger seat, his father quietly says, "Get the mail, Harry. Bring it inside to your mother. I'm going to the store. Your sister's covering for me there."

Only nodding, Harry does as he's told. With his winter jacket slung over his shoulders because the sleeve won't fit over his cast, he finagles open the car door and walks to the mailbox at the curb. After pulling out a handful of envelopes and flyers, he snaps the mailbox closed, walks up the stone walkway to the front door and goes inside.

But the silence there, too, and the awkwardness of using only one hand to maneuver the door, and the mail, and his jacket, and the sight of his father driving off? None of it compares to the weight of his regret. It's heavy and it stings, through and through. Harry let his father down, but good.

After talking a little with his also-disappointed mother, Harry settles in the tufted armchair beside the fireplace. Exhausted and sitting alone, one by one he opens the mailbox cards. His left-hand fingers extending from the cast hold the envelopes, while his right hand manages to tear each one open and pull out the holiday cards. It's the usual fare: Christmas greetings from a cousin, from an aunt and uncle, one from the Davis family's Victorian—where Harry's sure Pete is as annoyed as his own father.

Finally, Harry opens the last envelope. It's like he's looking at a painting of Addison itself when he pulls out the card and sees a watercolor of snowfall against a red, countryside barn. He can almost hear the hush of the moment captured. When he opens the card, a small square photograph drops out. It's a close-up of a teenage girl wearing a paisley-print, velour blazer over a brown turtleneck. Her blonde hair is layered; her gold hoop earrings glimmer; a locket hangs from a chain around her neck. But he doesn't recognize the girl's face, so instead he turns to the message written beneath the card's holiday verse:

Had my high school yearbook picture taken. Here's one for you, Lorrie. (I wore the necklace you gave me.) Merry Christmas to you and Allan.

Sadie

Harry looks at the photograph again, then drops the card in his lap and shakes his head.

"Ma!" he calls out toward the kitchen. "Didn't you ever write to this girl?"

21

"What girl?" his mother asks as she walks into the living room with a towel in hand.

Harry reads the name in the card again. "Sadie. She sent another card to …" He looks at the envelope. "Lorrie and Allan."

"Oh! I keep forgetting. I always plan to drop her a note after the holidays. But with running the store, it gets so busy and, well, the weeks and months go by." His mother walks closer while wiping her hands on that dishtowel. "She say anything this year?"

"Not much. Had her high school yearbook picture taken." Harry hands his mother the photograph.

Linda takes the picture, and then the card, too. She reads it quietly. "What a nice girl. If I'd known she was so young, just a child, really … Well, I hate to let her down." She tucks the yearbook picture and snowy barn card into the envelope, then walks to the Queen Anne end table on the other side of the room. "This year," she says while opening the table's small drawer. "This year, I'll definitely let her know."

"Ma," Harry says then.

His mother looks over her shoulder at him.

"What can I do to make it up to Pop?" he asks.

"Well. What's done is done." She sits on the sofa, towel still in her hands. "There's not much you can do now, wearing that cast. Which is too bad, because it's his busiest time of year, Harry, and Dad was counting on your help. But with a broken wrist, you can't work the soda fountain. Can't run the register. Can't gift-wrap." His mother shrugs and stands, heading to the kitchen again where some pot of soup simmers on the stovetop. The aroma drifts through the house. "Maybe just help keep things in order. Dust a little," she calls back. "Wipe things down in the store so things look nice for the customers."

"That's it?"

His mother turns and stops in the doorway. "You made a mistake, Harry. And mistakes are costly. In more ways than one. Now come have a sandwich I made for you, then get some rest. You've been up all night."

With a glance at the wall clock, Harry's surprised it's late morning already. "I guess I should grab a few hours' sleep."

"After your lunch," his mother says, motioning him to the kitchen. "I put an extra pillow on your bed, too, so you can prop your cast on it."

Not saying much more, Harry finishes his chicken club sandwich in the quiet kitchen, before heading down the hallway and closing his bedroom door behind him.

four

The Fourth Winter

HARRY CATCHES HIS REFLECTION IN the mirror at Joel's Bar and Grille. He does a double take, actually, as he sits there at the crowded bar. That guy in the mirror, is it really him? The one wearing a navy Henley sweater over a button-down shirt. Harry's celebrating turning twenty-one tonight, so he looks for some change in his appearance. Some adult trait. Some wisdom in his eyes. Drawing a hand along his jaw, he feels a shadow of whiskers there. And his dark hair verges on unkempt, in need of a trim at the very least. But it's casual, and easygoing, just like the night out with his friends. They're sitting at a large, round table over on the side of the room.

Waiting to order a second tray of cheese nachos, Harry glances around for the waitress. Miniature Christmas trees twinkle at either end of the bar. Swags of silver garland are strung above it, and rocking holiday tunes play on the jukebox. The joint is jumping as folks ring in the season with a drink, a dance or two, a kiss beneath sprigs of mistletoe hanging here and there.

It's the perfect place for a birthday party, too, with all those good vibes going on. Though his birthday was earlier in the fall, Harry's friends wanted to get together and commemorate this one. With everyone away at college, or working jobs, they missed the chance to toast Harry's day when it actually happened.

It's a big one, they'd told him earlier today. *Twenty-one, man. All grown up now. A legit adult. Let's go out and toast it.*

And when Harry eventually returns to his table with the nachos, it's shoulder slaps and back claps all around. Actually, the night passes in the same whirlwind as his first twenty-one years of school and Little League and summers. Of family holidays and birthdays and backyard barbecues. Tonight's hours are the same blur of toasts, and of reminiscing with his boyhood friends, and of sitting close with his college girlfriend. Tess had come home with him for a few days before Christmas to meet his parents. They set up a spare room for her and are as smitten with Tess as he is.

So there is a change for Harry. There's love now. For his friends, too. Nate lets on that he's actually going to propose to his girlfriend for Christmas. When someone asks if he's crazy, being in his early twenties and committing like that, he say yes. Crazy in love.

That's how Harry feels all night long. Crazy in love. With Tess. With his life. With his New England hometown. With Christmas. As they all eat good food, and laugh, and dance to the jumpin' jukebox, as Harry sneaks in a few mistletoe kisses with Tess in his arms, yes, he is crazy in love with everything.

So much so that he doesn't want the feeling to end. Long after he and Tess are back at his parents' home, long after everyone's turned in, after he's said goodnight to Tess, Harry sits alone beside the fireplace. The living room is dark, except for the illuminated Christmas tree. Its tiny white lights cast a dim glow, leaving soft shadows, giving the room that look one might recall in nostalgic memories. He could sit here for hours, lingering in the night, remembering the laughs with his friends, the stolen mistletoe kisses with his girl, the good cheer.

Looking around the room, Harry notices a pile of Christmas cards his mother must've opened and left on the coffee table. He reaches for them and thumbs through the greetings by the light of the tree. *Love to all. Wishing you the merriest!* And, *Hello to the family.* And, *All best for the New Year!* Warm messages from relatives, friends, neighbors.

Except for one.

Harry shakes his head with a small smile as he reads the name written in the card, flips to the front and looks at the white silhouette of a prancing reindeer leaping across a red background. Then he opens the card again.

Dear Lorrie and Allan,

Merry Christmas from my dorm room! Just had our first snow on campus, it's so pretty.

Hope all is well … Sadie

Harry runs his finger across the inked words, then tucks the card back in its envelope, gets up and drops it in the end table drawer with the few others accumulated there.

When he sits near the tree again, he sees that outside the living room's paned windows, a light snow falls here, too.

five

The Fifth Winter

HARRY'S EVERY WISH HAS COME true this year; there's no denying it. He graduated from college. His internship in the finance department of a Boston tech firm turned into a permanent job, one paying enough for him to land a studio apartment in the city. Tess is in Boston, too, finishing up her junior year of college. Really, he's on top of the world this Christmas.

But.

But, but, but. What is it they say? For every door that opens, another closes? That must be why Harry's feeling a little melancholy this trip home. Working full-time in Boston now, gone are the one-month winter breaks from school. Breaks when he visited his parents for weeks on end in their country bungalow in Addison. Easy weeks when he worked long days in the general store selling light bulbs and jigsaw puzzles; chocolate brownies and dishtowels; wind chimes and cutting boards and sweatshirts. Breaks when he worked side by side with his father.

Now? Now those times during the past four years seem like a dream. A fond memory. The image you might see on a Christmas card … storefront windows lined with cottony faux snow; a train set chugging along the tracks behind the glass; folks bundled up in the cold, stopping in for hand-crafted gifts, and wrapping paper, and cards, all while calling out, *Hey, Harry! Good to see you. Happy holidays, Harry.*

This year, his three *days* home leave little time for more than a brief stop at the store. He helps his father for an hour or two on Christmas Eve day. Harry wraps gifts and serves complimentary hot Christmas cocoa at the soda fountain to any last-minute shoppers.

This year, he barely has time to sit in his favorite living room chair beside the tree. Barely has time to see a friend. To catch up with his mother and sister, Emma. To read the stack of holiday cards that arrived all during December.

He finally does that on Christmas night. His aunts and uncles and cousins had put on their wool coats and caps before saying long goodbyes and giving second hugs at the front door. His father turned in early, because it's always a busy week at the store with lots of visitors in town for the holidays. Fresh coffee will be percolating at the crack of dawn for customers lined up on the swivel stools. And a few minutes ago, his mother got her movie camera and filmed the Christmas tree twinkling in the dimly lit living room at day's end, like she does every year. Now, his sister and mother tidy up the kitchen.

That's when Harry sits alone in the living room chair, cards in his lap, and first just looks at that Christmas tree. After a few minutes, he gives a long sigh and turns to the cards. *Holiday greetings to the Danes!* And, *Wishing you all a Christmas filled with joy.* And, *Hello to the family.* Happy little notes fill the messages from relatives and friends. Some are typed on glossy family-photo Christmas cards, others penned in traditional store-bought cards.

One, though, is still sealed in its unopened envelope. Harry tears the flap and pulls out the card. The woodland picture on it is of a snowy footbridge over a babbling brook. He opens the card and finds that his eyes go right to the note written beneath the card's verse.

> *Sad news this Christmas, Lorrie. We lost Mom in May. It's just not the same without her. Mom and I always wrote our holiday cards together, so now I'm continuing on for her.*
>
> *Sending love,*
> *Sadie*

Harry reads the note again, then flips to the snowy footbridge. He wonders why his mother hasn't gotten in touch with this Sadie—who's been sending Christmas cards to this house's previous owners for years now. "Hey, Ma," Harry calls over his shoulder.

"In a minute, Harry," his mother calls back. "Let me get these platters put away."

Harry waits, then reads the sad note from Sadie again before slipping the card back into its envelope addressed to Lorrie and Allan. After giving another glance toward the kitchen, he stands and walks across the shadowy living room to the small Queen Anne end table. There, he opens the drawer and drops Sadie's card in with the others that are still there after all this time. His hand brushes across them before he turns away.

Moments later, his mother comes into the living room. "Did you need something?"

"What?" Harry asks from where he now looks out the frosty paned window onto the winter night. "No. No, it was nothing," he says. Says *instead* of bringing up Sadie's sad loss this year, and her mistakenly sent cards. Maybe tomorrow he'll nudge his mother to finally get in touch with her. "It's just that, well … I had a nice Christmas, Ma."

"We had a nice holiday, too. It's wonderful having you and Emma home like this," his mother tells him before rattling pots and opening cabinets in the kitchen again.

Harry grabs his coat and hat from the front closet. "Think I'll take a walk around the block," he says while putting his arms in the coat sleeves in the kitchen doorway. "Walk off some of this turkey."

"Don't be too late!" his mother calls out as the front door closes behind him.

Outside, snow crunches beneath his boots. In front yards, country lampposts are snowcapped. Lights twinkle on low shrubs. Wreaths and boughs of greenery decorate porches and doorways. And golden lamplight spills from all the homes' windows on this still night.

"I'll see you in January, son," his father says at the front door the next evening. "Thanks for the tickets. Best Christmas present ever."

"No problem, Pop." Harry zips his jacket, picks up his overnight duffel and walks out to the bungalow's front porch. Snow is falling, dusting the porch railings and the shrubs draped with white lights. "You always liked hockey. We'll have a guys' night out on the town. Go to the Bruins game, grab something to eat, have a beer or two."

"Looking forward to it, Harry."

As Harry settles into his car, he sees his father step outside onto the porch. The house is aglow; the Christmas tree still twinkles in the living room windows; a burgundy ribbon flutters on a balsam wreath hanging on the wood-planked front door. Seeing it all—home, his father waving in the illumination of the porch light— Harry feels unexpectedly sad. He's not sure why. His life in Boston suits him just fine—from his amazing job in the city, to beautiful Tess and their New Year's Eve plans. And the Christmas holiday at home was perfect. Busy, but festive as can be.

Still. Pulling out of the driveway and waving his gloved hand out the window as his father closes the door behind him, Harry misses him already.

Actually, Harry's kind of missed his father the whole time he was here. How could he not this winter, with only a three-day visit.

Harry missed his father during the sparse hours he worked beside him in the general store this time—instead of the month they were used to.

Missed him when they swept an inch of powdery snow off the front sidewalk Christmas morning—instead of the piles they'd clear during Harry's winter breaks.

Missed him when he sat across from him at the holiday table during their one meal together—instead of their countless evening dinners at the kitchen farm table. "Dark meat or white, Harry?" his father asked yesterday while carving the turkey.

But mostly? Mostly Harry's finding it hard to leave since reading Sadie's sad Christmas note last night. He gives a last look in the rearview mirror, right before the snow-covered country bungalow fades out of sight.

six

The Sixth Winter

H ARRY." IT'S THE FIRST WORD from his mother when Harry answers the phone in his Boston apartment. No *Hello*. No *How are you?* She says just his name, before asking, "Can you come home early for Christmas?"

"Oh, Ma," Harry says.

He turns to Tess sitting on his sofa. She wears a soft gray sweater over dark jeans. And Harry falls in love with her more and more each day. Tess had set a tray of cheese and crackers on the coffee table, after they'd hung gold ornaments and white lights on a small tabletop Christmas tree. It was the tiniest one they'd found on a tree lot two blocks over. *My mother*, he mouthes to her while holding the phone to his ear.

"Tess just started winter break," Harry says into the phone then. "I was going with her to her parents' this weekend. Spending a few days with her family before I head to Addison."

"Harry."

That's it. His mother says nothing more. A few silent seconds pass before her quiet, urgent voice reaches his ear.

"It's Dad."

⚬

Once his father is moved out of the intensive care unit after the open-heart surgery, Harry still waits. He wants his father to be more comfortable, and to have regained enough lung capacity to talk easily. He wants his pop to get better.

Maybe this will help, Harry thinks four days post surgery when he walks into his father's hospital room. It's early, and his mother and sister aren't there yet. They've been visiting in shifts so that someone is with his father most of the time. Helping in any way they can. Walking with him in the hospital hallway. Handing him get-well cards, or a comb, or a cup with a straw to sip from.

"Hey, Pop," Harry says when he pulls a chair alongside the bed. His father wears diamond-print hospital-issued pajamas. Equipment is wired to monitor his vital signs. Harry hopes that his plan will alleviate some of his father's worries. "You feeling a little better today?"

"I am, Harry," his father tells him while slightly nodding.

"You're looking better, too," Harry says, moving aside his father's slippers and pulling his chair closer to the bed. "The staff treating you okay? Taking care of you?"

"They're the best. Doing whatever they can."

"Okay, that's good. I'll give you a shave this morning. Would you like that?"

"I would."

"In a while, though. I brought some Christmas cards from home. The mailbox was full of them yesterday, and I thought I'd open them here. Cheer you up some." Harry pulls the handful of cards from a small bag and sets them on the edge of the bed. Slowly, sitting there in the hospital room with nurses breezing in and out, and monitors humming, and his father silently watching him, he opens each envelope. Funny how the festive cards strike him differently this year. The snowy woodland scenes, and poinsettias, and Santas and sprigs of holly and berries. As merry as Christmas has been in the past, this year, it's actually solemn.

Even so, Harry reads the holiday greetings sent their way. The cards' sentiments are toned down this December. There's concern, but hope, in many of the personal messages. Harry reads each card's rhyming verse, then each penned line added beneath them.

Our prayers are with Norman.
A restful Christmas to you all!
Feel better, Norm.

After holding up each card for his father to see, Harry puts them back in his bag. Halfway through, he lifts a Christmas postcard from among the envelopes. The postcard photograph is unmistakably of London's Westminster Abbey, its gothic towers reaching to a pale blue sky. He flips over the card and silently reads the easy-flowing cursive crossing the card's back.

Studying abroad this semester, Lorrie. Happy Christmas from jolly old England!

Sadie

Uncertain that his father even knows about this Sadie address mix-up, Harry slips the postcard back in the bag and finishes reading the remaining cards instead. At this point, he'd drop Sadie a line himself, except there's no return address on a postcard.

"Listen, Pop," Harry says while setting aside the bag of Christmas cards. "There's something I want to talk to you about. I don't know if now's a good time, but maybe it is."

"Everything okay with you, son?"

"With me? Sure. It's you I'm worried about. So, I don't know … But maybe this will help you get better, what I'm going to say."

"What is it, Harry? You seem serious."

Harry looks at his father. He leans close and lightly claps his father's jaw, then stands and walks to the window. Outside, the sky is gray. Snow is coming. When Harry turns back, he does it. He does the one and only thing he can to help his father recover.

"I'll take care of the store for you, Pop."

"What?"

"The general store," Harry says. "I'll run things there so you can focus on getting better. You've got a long road ahead of you. Exercise, diet, doctor appointments. And you'll be tired. So this way, you don't have to worry about the business. I'll be working there."

"But you're not familiar with the vendors, and how I—"

"I know enough. You taught me well, on all my college breaks. And summer vacations. You can count on me."

"But your mother said she'll handle it. And I have good help."

"Part-time help, which isn't enough. And Mom? She needs to be taking care of *you*. Driving you to your appointments. Taking walks with you. Cooking healthy food." Now Harry returns to his bedside chair. His father looks tired. The surgery took its toll on him. It has on all of them. Harry leans close again. "So listen. I gave my notice at the office."

His father says nothing. Instead, he looks away, blinking back tears—Harry can't miss that.

"You worked hard to get that job, Harry." When his father finally says it, he's shaking his head.

"Eh. Plenty of jobs out there. I can always get another one," Harry says offhandedly. "And that general store is your *everything*, Pop. Everything. Not to mention, you're a fixture in this town. So I'll keep the business afloat while you and Mom get through this. It's what I want to do. Manage it for you."

"What about Tess?"

"Tess? She's okay with this. We talked about it. And Boston's not too far, so we'll manage long-distance for a while. I'll drive there; she'll come here. We're good."

"You're sure?" his father asks, his voice barely more than a whisper.

"I am. And don't worry. It's only temporary. Until you're better and have the okay to work again."

"And your mother. Does she know you quit your job in Boston?"

"No. And she doesn't know I broke the lease on my apartment there, either. But it doesn't matter. The decision's made, Pop." Harry stands then, and leans down to give his father a hug around all the bandaging and wires and tubes. But he does it, getting his arms around his father's shoulders and holding him close. "I'm moving back home."

seven

The Seventh Winter

HARRY'S TRIED SEVERAL TIMES ALREADY this morning. At ten thirty, he tries again. Tries to flip the general store's *Open* sign to *Closed*. He makes it as far as the door, which he opens to get a better look at the blizzard blowing outside. Though the wind-whipped snow makes it hard to see, Harry squints out at Main Street—which is nearly impassable in the foot of fresh snow. The plowed snowbanks are twice as deep, making the situation worse.

Beyond, The Green is blanketed in white, too. Even the town's soaring Christmas tree is barely discernible. Its colored lights only softly glimmer in a blush beneath the heavy white snow. At the colonial homes and farmhouses surrounding The Green, more snow reaches up to front-porch railings; parked cars are mere white mounds huddled in driveways; smoke swirls from snowcapped chimney tops.

And that wind! In all his twenty-four years, Harry's never heard anything like it. He quickly closes the door—but the wind's howling whistle makes its way right inside. Just as he's finally about to flip the store's sign to *Closed* and lock up, something comes into view. There's a motion outside. A dark shadow behind all those swirling snowflakes. Someone is bent into the wind, one arm raised as he calls out to Harry.

"Thank goodness you're open," the man says as he steps inside onto the black-and-white checkerboard floor. It's Tom Riley, an attorney who lives crosstown in the apple-orchard development. The wind blows a swirl of flakes inside with him. "And merry Christmas, Harry!"

"Same to you, Tom. Merry Christmas."

"Surprised to see you open today. Dane's General Store? Always closed on the holiday."

"With the storm coming, I spent the night here on the cot, back in the office," Harry explains. "Wanted to stay ahead of the shoveling and keep the front walkway cleared."

"I'm sure your father appreciates that. You really stepped up to the plate this year, while Norm was on the mend."

Harry nods. "Wasn't intending to be open for business today, but folks must notice the lights on and it's actually been busy."

"On Christmas morning?"

"You bet. People braving the storm for last-minute things. Emergency items."

"Me, too. Need a thermometer, Harry. Our little one, Kat, she's running a temp."

As the phone rings, Harry points Tom to the wooden shelves in the wellness row. After telling the caller the store's open for a little while longer, he tunes a portable radio to the local station before Tom stops at the register.

"Picked up some batteries, too," Tom says as he sets them on the counter. "Might lose our electricity, with all that snow weighing down the power lines."

"Good idea," Harry tells him as he bags the items. "Hope your daughter feels better. Gets to enjoy her presents from Santa."

"You closing up soon?" Tom walks to the door. "Heading home to your family?" he calls over his shoulder.

As the phone rings again, just as another customer enters the store in a swirl of more snow and wind, Harry simply shrugs and waves off Tom.

"Dane's General," Harry says into the store phone. "Yes, we're open this morning." When he hangs up, the phone rings again, right away. "Dane's," Harry says. "Yeah, got a few flashlights left."

"That's what I came for, too," the waiting customer says. His coat collar's flipped up, his hat's covered in snow, and he blows warm air into his fisted fingers. "Power's out on the west side of town."

And the rest of Christmas Day? It passes in the same swirl as the blowing snow outside the frosted windowpanes. The phone rings; customers, familiar and not, bustle into the store. Cheeks are rosy; mittens are snow-caked; and a distinct *thump-thump* always sounds, right before the door opens. It's the *thump-thump* of boots being stamped on the porch floor to shake off the snow before folks come inside.

All the while, the hands of the clock spin again and again with each passing hour. As Harry rings out his customers, and pours steaming hot chocolate at the soda fountain, and hangs up the ringing phone, the talk in the store is lively.

Snowing like the dickens this year! Straight out of a picture book, this holiday is.
You missing Christmas, Harry?
Little bit, George.
Family keeping a plate warm for you?
Hope so, Frank.
Have any blankets? Power's out at my place, and it's getting chilly.
Over in the corner, Mrs. DeMartino.
Your father around? Or are you running the show today?
It's just me, Mr. Dawson.
Hold onto your hat, the local weatherman Leo Sterling says on the portable radio. *Wind'll be blowing this way and that!*
He's not kidding, Harry. Will you make it home for Christmas dinner?
Trying to. Hello, Dane's General Store.

Harry finally manages a look at his watch, then walks to the paned windows edged in windblown snow.

Falling two inches an hour, Leo Sterling's voice booms from the radio, *that mighty white snow will surely tower!*

Leo wasn't kidding. After all the customers have made their purchases and braved the storm again to get

43

themselves home that afternoon, Harry finally flips the *Open* sign to *Closed*. From the looks of the, yes, the *towering* piles of snow lining the street and the snowflakes still falling in the late-day hour, there's no way he'll be able to drive home. So with a long breath, he dims the lights, wipes down the soda fountain counter and answers the once-again ringing phone.

"Harry?"

"Tess." Harry's eyes briefly drop closed. "Oh, Tess."

"Merry Christmas, Harry." Her voice is soft, and a little sad, too.

"Same to … It's just that it's been crazy here. I haven't had a chance … well … Merry Christmas, Tess."

"I called your parents' house. They said you're *working* today?"

"I am. I mean, I wasn't going to, but the storm, and—"

"But what about Christmas?" Tess asks from her parents' Beacon Hill row house in Boston. "You're not even spending it at home?"

Harry looks out at the still-howling blizzard. Tiny, icy flakes tap at the windowpanes. The garland wrapped around the porch posts blows in the wind. "No. I just couldn't make it," Harry says.

"But you're still coming here for New Year's, right?"

"Wouldn't miss it."

"Do you think you can come a few days early? Maybe we can go ice-skating, and there's a show I'd like to see."

"I can't promise anything, Tess," Harry says with a glance around the store. Shelves are now only partially stocked with assorted Dane's General Store goods: coffee mugs and can openers and paper products. Inventories are running low, and a delivery truck is due here first thing in the morning, come snow or sunshine. "It's hard to get away. My dad's not back to full-time, so we're busy."

"Try?" she quietly asks.

And he knows. Knows by the softness of her words that she's disappointed he's not with her in Boston for the holidays.

"Tess. You know I'm helping out my parents with the store. They still need me to pitch in."

"But it's been a year now, that you're working there. And we hardly see each other." A pause, then, "I'm sorry you missed Christmas today," Tess whispers, before telling him that *she* misses him, too.

What Harry doesn't say is that the store was actually chock-*full* of Christmas today. That he'd plugged in the lights on the countertop Christmas tree, and set a basket of free candy canes beside it.

That each and every customer who made their way through the fierce storm and brushed off their snowy coat as they came through the door had nothing but good cheer and thankfulness that Harry kept the general store open.

That many folks chalked festive greetings on the store's blackboard.

That for each pair of fluffy socks and each flashlight and jigsaw puzzle and jar of peanuts and candle and stainless-steel peeler and package of throat lozenges he sold, there came a pat on the shoulder, a hug, a warm holiday greeting.

That at one point, there was a spontaneous storewide *Jingle Bells* sing-along.

After tidying the picked-over shelves and sweeping the checkerboard floor, Harry tunes the radio to some light Christmas music. He shuts off the store's main lights, too, but leaves on the white twinkling lights wrapped around the porch posts outside. Taking the radio with him then, he settles in the back office again. When he came into work yesterday, Christmas Eve day, he didn't plan on staying overnight. Not until he heard that Addison would take a direct Christmas Day hit from the blizzard.

So his mother had dropped off a care package last night, as he weathered the storm and kept an eye on the store. *Pajamas, slippers. A little something to eat tomorrow*, she'd told him. *And a few treats to while away the time.*

Harry takes the wrapped food from the dorm-sized refrigerator now and uncovers turkey slices arranged with all the trimmings, gravy on the side. After heating the plates in the microwave, he settles at the office desk, clears some space and digs in. The portable radio plays holiday tunes beside him. He listens to voices crooning about being home, and taking snowy sleigh rides, and fireplaces glowing, and marshmallows toasting.

"Well," Harry says to no one but himself. He folds back his flannel shirt cuffs, then forks a piece of turkey and drags it through some stuffing and cranberry sauce. *"Merry Christmas, Harry Dane,"* he whispers before lifting the food to his mouth.

Would it have been nice to be home and eating this dinner with his family? Sure. Or to be with Tess, sitting cozy beside her at her parents' dining room table? Of course.

Instead, he had a Dane's General Store holiday. One

he's about to top off with brownies. With the sweetest, creamiest brownies this side of the Connecticut River. Because if there's one thing Harry's learned after years of working behind the counter at Dane's General Store, it's this: When the store is busy, set aside a couple of Bea's Brownies before they're cleared out.

And he did, today. So after forking every morsel and crumb of his turkey dinner, he rinses and dries the dishes before grabbing the rest of his care package from home. His mother had tucked a few things into the bag for him: warm socks, a crossword puzzle, and any Christmas cards that came in yesterday's mail.

I know how you like opening the holiday cards, Harry, her note says. *Saved these for you!*

First things first, though. And first is to unwrap one of those townwide-coveted brownies. Then, and only then, does Harry lean back in the office chair and open the envelopes. An old neighbor from across town wishes them well. His father's brother and wife sent a photograph of their beagle sitting in front of a roaring fireplace. A longtime store customer who's since moved away writes how much he misses Christmas shopping at Dane's General Store.

Biting into a chocolate-chip-filled brownie right as the office light flickers in a gust of wind, Harry finally opens the last envelope and begins reading the penned note inside the card.

Began my last year of college. Met a really nice guy—

"Wait a minute," Harry says aloud as he first flips over the card, then grabs up its envelope to give it a good scrutiny, only to find that it's addressed to that Lorrie and Allan. "Oh, man. Not again," he says, shaking his head before giving the card a second look. On its front is a picture of a snowman with coal buttons and a red scarf wrapped around its neck. He wears a top hat tipped on a jaunty angle and holds a piece of sheet music as though singing a Christmas carol.

But it's the note inside that Harry lingers with longest. *Began my last year of college*, he reads again. The woman's easy cursive is written on an angle beneath the card's rhyming verse.

> *Met a really nice guy this fall. We're going to a Christmas concert at the campus auditorium tonight. I'm well, Lorrie. Hope you and Allan are, too.*
>
> *Warmly,*
> *Sadie*

"Oh, Sadie, Sadie, Sadie," Harry quietly says. A wooden shelf beside the desk is lined with various store ledgers. Harry moves them to the side and neatly lines up his four Christmas cards on the shelf, too. After turning down the blanket on the cramped office cot in the corner, he looks back at the cards again.

Well, looks at the one snowman card and turns up his hands. From the radio comes a sentimental song about being home for the holidays. "Hope you had a nice Christmas, Sadie," Harry says. "Wherever it might have been."

eight

The Eighth Winter

HARRY'S FIRST SURPRISE IS THE phone call that comes into the store. It's Tess. She wants to meet him for dinner.

"Tonight?" Harry asks while ringing out a customer with one hand, the phone held to his ear with the other.

"Yes. I got out of work early."

"You're driving here from Boston?"

"I will. Meet me at the restaurant? Cedar Ridge Tavern?"

Harry agrees as he hands the customer her change. The store is busy. Shoppers look for twinkling lights to string on their lampposts and around porch eaves. Couples pick out Christmas ornaments for their trees. Families buy candy canes, and sweet peppermint bark, and silver tinsel garland. Even though it's only the first Friday of December, annual decorating sprees have begun. Brass window candles and pinecone napkin rings and tartan tablecloths and snow globes and miniature nutcrackers for holiday mantels? They all fly off the shelves. The crowds are big enough to extend the store hours all month.

Harry cuts out early, though, leaving his parents to man the register.

"Take the van," his father, Norm, tells him.

"The van?" Harry stops as he's about to leave through the store's rear door. "Why?"

"You can make a delivery for me on your way home. Mrs. Crenshaw, over on Old Willow Road, needs her cheese platter delivery. She's having a holiday party tomorrow. Then gas up the van before you bring it back tonight."

So Harry does. He stops at the Crenshaw house and trots up to her front door. Problem is, Mrs. Crenshaw doesn't just take the two cheese platters from him. When her little dog, Pepper, scoots out the door, Mrs. Crenshaw comes out, too. And before you know it, she's got Harry decorating for her holiday party, stringing Christmas lights around her front door.

Holiday parties ... Christmas decorating. Driving home, Harry wonders where the months have gone. One thing's for sure. After spending the past two years helping out his father by managing the general store, it's been tough on Tess, this long-distance relationship. So if a dinner here and there keeps the spark going until he can turn the store over to his father again and return to Boston, Harry's all for it. He stops home for a quick shower, and after dragging a hand across a shadow of whiskers on his jaw, skips a shave. Instead, he puts on black jeans and a fisherman sweater, grabs his leather bomber and leaves for the restaurant. Oh, and he does one more thing in the dusky evening light—checks the mailbox and tosses any envelopes and flyers on the van's front seat.

It's a good thing, too. With no sign of Tess at the restaurant, he's got a few minutes to kill. So while waiting in the parked van, Harry goes through the mail. An outdoor clothing catalog first, then the envelopes. Mixed in with a few bills are some early Christmas cards. Those, he opens. First is a card from an old coworker in Boston, now married and writing that the new year will be bringing a new baby, too. Harry sets that card aside, checks for Tess through the windshield, then opens the second card—a red envelope addressed to Lorrie and Allan. This time, he recognizes the sender's name.

"Ah, Sadie," he whispers as he slips the envelope flap open. "Sadie, Sadie, Sadie. What are you up to this year?" He pulls out the card and skips right to the penned note at the bottom.

> *Graduated from college this May, Lorrie. Remember all those years ago when you would help me with my homework? Thinking of you and Allan.*
>
> *Merry Christmas!*
> *Sadie*

A sudden *tap-tap-tap* on the driver's window has Harry jump.

"Tess!" he says, tossing Sadie's card aside and getting out of the van. Tess waits for him at the curb. She's wearing a quilted jacket with a fur-lined hood, and has on suede knee-high boots over her jeans. Her auburn hair is down; her silver hoop earrings shimmer. "Tess," Harry says again after locking the van door and giving her a quick kiss. "I didn't see you pull up."

Together, they walk into Cedar Ridge Tavern. Harry asks Tess about the drive from Boston as the hostess leads them past the dark walnut bar to a tiny table beside a stone fireplace. On a Friday night, the dimly lit dining room is packed, filled with lively conversation and clinking silverware and toasts ringing in the holiday season. Once a waiter takes their wine order and leaves them with two dinner menus, Harry looks at Tess. Looks at her across the candlelit table, at her gentle eyes watching his. At her silky hair tucked behind an ear as she pulls off her leather gloves. Looks at her and thinks this could be *their* place, this restaurant, with its flames snapping in the fireplace and its evocative lighting.

Yes, this could actually be the place where he eventually proposes to her. Maybe on a snowy winter night, right before Christmas, with snowflakes tapping at the windows as they sit so close.

For now, he clasps Tess' hands in his, leans across the small tabletop and kisses her again. "It's *so* good to see you," he tells her. "I've really missed you."

"Harry," Tess says, softly.

Harry notices that. Notices how softly she says his name. There's something different about it. Different about the way she said it with the smallest of smiles on her face. It's the sort of expression that has him tip his head and start to ask her if everything's okay.

Until their waiter interrupts with their wineglasses and says he'll be back shortly to take their dinner orders.

When Harry nods to him, then turns to Tess again, she's carefully slipping out of her quilted jacket and hanging it over the back of her chair. She does this all, he notices, without looking at him. So he lifts his glass and raises it to her. "A toast, Tess? To us being together tonight?"

Tess raises her glass, but doesn't clink it to his. Instead, she whispers, "Harry."

Harry sets down his wine without drinking any. "What's wrong?"

"Harry, I had to see you in person." Tess takes a long swallow of her wine before setting down her glass, too. "Had to tell you in person."

"Tell me? Tell me what?"

She sits very still as her eyes fill with tears. "It's over, Harry."

"What are you talking about?"

"It's over. We are. I can't do this anymore."

"This?"

"This ... Back and forth between two states. Trying to make things work. Make *us* work."

Harry pulls his chair in closer. The first surprise of the day was Tess' phone call earlier. He looks at her sad eyes now as the day's second surprise arrives—she's leaving him. "But Tess." He turns up his hands, at a loss for words. "You mean, you're breaking up with me?"

"I am."

"Why?"

Again she sips her wine. Her eyes never leave his.

"Are you seeing someone else?" Harry asks.

She shakes her head, no. "But maybe ... Maybe I want to be able to."

"I don't get it. What happened?"

"That's the hard part, Harry." She briefly clasps his hand. "What happened is you. You being your wonderful self and helping to save your father's store after his heart surgery. Your parents are very lucky. Because you're generous and kind and loving, which makes this all the harder to explain."

Harry leans back and crosses his arms over his chest. "Well try, Tess. Because I thought things were serious between us."

Beside them in the dimly lit room, the fire crackles. Crystal glasses sparkle. Voices rise and fall. And there it is again, Tess' smile. That small smile that says it all. Says there's no going back—they're done.

"Harry. The problem is this. You'll *never* leave here."

"Here?"

"Addison."

"How can you say that? You know my father's better. He's back to work all the time now."

"Has been for some time, too," Tess says.

"That's right."

"Which is my point. Your dad's been running the store again for almost a year, and you've made no move to come back to Boston. I've asked you to, but there's always one reason or another keeping you here in Connecticut. The store needs a new van. Or is open longer hours. Or you have meetings scheduled with local vendors." She pauses, swiping away an escaped tear. "Addison is *your* home, not mine. My home, my family and my job are in Boston, Harry. I belong *there*. And I know now."

"Know what?"

"That as much as I want it to, things will never work between us."

"We'll *make* it work. We just need more time."

Tess shakes her head. "Harry, I'm twenty-three already, and you're twenty-five. We're done with college, and I stayed in Boston." She gives a small smile. "But you ended up here. Which I totally get. You love Addison. It's written all over you. This is your home and I could never ask you to leave. It would break your heart."

"That's not true, Tess."

She only nods, briefly.

"Tess." He slides his chair around the table to sit beside her. "I thought we'd get married."

"No, Harry," she whispers as she reaches up and touches his hair. Her eyes actually drink in the sight of him, then. All while silent tears slip from her eyes. "That's why I'm here. Because I thought that, too. That this Christmas, you might actually ask me to marry you. Maybe buy a diamond ring. And I'm telling you not to." She takes his face in her hands and kisses him the gentlest of kisses. "You're a good man, Harry," she softly says as she gathers her gloves and bag. "But you and I? We're not meant to be. We live in different worlds." With her quilted coat slung over her arm, she squeezes his shoulder, bends low and whispers, "Goodbye, Harry," before pressing past him to the door.

Harry turns and watches her go. He almost calls out, but doesn't. Instead, he moves his chair back to the other side of the table and sits again. Sits alone beside the fire. Two glasses of wine and two menus are on the table. He lifts his wineglass and takes a long sip. He takes another then, too, but never looks toward the restaurant's door. Never gets up to go after Tess. Because the thing is? As much as he doesn't want to admit it, he knows she's right.

"Will your friend be returning?" the waiter suddenly asks as he approaches the table.

"No. She won't."

"Will you still be having dinner?"

"Not tonight. No."

"Oh, sorry to hear that." The waiter looks from him, to the door, then back to Harry. "I'll get these out of your way," he says while lifting the menus off the table and leaving Harry alone there.

After the waiter goes, Harry finishes the rest of his wine in one long swallow. A quiet moment passes when he just sits by himself. Finally, he puts on his bomber jacket and drops enough money on the table to cover his tab before walking out into the December night.

nine

The Ninth Winter

THE HUSHED VOICES GIVE IT away that afternoon. Something's wrong. When customers see a familiar face, they hurry over, lean close with concern. Whisper. Harry even notices that business slows. Usually Fridays in December are bustling. The door might as well be revolving, the way folks are in and out for various seasonal things. A wreath hook; extra plastic cups for a holiday party; a calendar for the new year; scissors and tape for gift-wrapping; or just a hot cocoa to warm up. Harry had come in at two to cover the late shift, and sent his father home to rest and have a good hot meal. The store would be busy tomorrow, with Santa scheduled to make an appearance.

But today, as the afternoon light wanes, there's a change in the air. Harry's never seen anything like it. In the store, shoppers' voices are low. And serious.

"Did you hear what happened, Harry?" a regular

customer finally asks at the register.

"No. What's going on, Arthur?"

The man talks quietly. "There was a drowning at the cove. A young girl."

"Oh, no. That's terrible! Today?"

"Just a while ago. After school got out."

"Who was it?" Harry asks. "Do you know?"

Arthur gives a slow nod. "Abby. Abby Cooper. You know Derek, from Cooper Hardware? His little girl."

Shaken by the tragedy, Harry pieces together the sad details by listening to folks telling the story. By hearing how Abby and a classmate were testing the ice to see if they could skate on the cove this weekend. The ice gave out, and both girls went under the frigid water. Harry hears how the fire department's water rescue team was able to save only one girl. Despite their underwater search, too many minutes passed before they found Abby. Once they finally did, none of their valiant efforts could revive her. She'd been under too long. They were too late.

As fewer and fewer customers come through the general store's door, each person is more somber than the last. Folks simply nod to Harry instead of chatting small talk. Or they pay for their items and quietly leave. It seems the entire town's heart has collectively broken on this one solemn afternoon.

The reverberations of Abby Cooper's drowning continue to reach Dane's General Store. Though open until eight o'clock today, by seven, there are no customers. The store is empty, leaving Harry with an eerie feeling. He walks to the door and looks out the window to Main Street. Storefronts are decorated, and the illuminated town tree on

The Green soars to the winter sky, but a darkness clouds it all. Harry looks out for a minute longer, then gets the straw broom from the back and begins sweeping the checkerboard floor. Every now and then, the bell over the door rings as a random customer stops in for a spool of thread; another for a screwdriver to assemble Christmas toys—a dollhouse, or bicycle and such.

"You hear the news, Harry?" one asks.

"I did. It's a shame, a crying shame."

The woman nods, takes her bag and leaves.

As Harry continues sweeping, the bell over the door rings once more. When he hears nothing—no voice greeting him, no shuffling of feet as the customer shops—Harry looks over his shoulder.

And looks again, when he sees that it's actually Derek Cooper there. His dark hair is a mess, his face exhausted, his posture defeated. The bottom of his jeans are damp—clinging to his legs near his work boots. On this freezing December day, he wears no coat. Standing there, Derek folds back the cuff of his flannel shirt first, glances out the window, then checks his watch.

"Derek," Harry says as he sets aside the broom and crosses the store. He takes Derek's hand, shakes it, and pulls him into a hug. "I am so sorry, my friend," Harry says while patting Derek's shoulder.

"I know. Thanks, Harry."

"Are you okay, man? Do you need something?"

Derek checks his watch again before glancing around the store. "Not sure."

"Anything. What can I get for you?"

"Don't really know. Just turned in here to get out of

the cold." Derek drags his hand through his hair. "Been a tough day." Another pause as he walks to the door, stops and looks out on the night. "Maybe … I don't know. Maybe I should get going."

Harry hears it, in Derek's voice. Hears the fatigue. The hoarse fatigue. Hears the grief. Hears the raspy result of some sorrow-filled weeping that had to have happened between now and, well, and then.

"Come on," Harry says as he puts his arm around Derek's shoulders and leads him to the soda fountain. He sees it, Derek's confusion; his quiet shock at the turn of the day. "Sit for a minute," Harry tells him. "Get your bearings, guy. Warm up."

Derek does. He sits on a stool, leans his arms on the counter, drops his head and just breathes. When he does, Harry rushes over to the door and locks it before flipping the *Open* sign to *Closed*. He also shuts off the outside lights and dims the interior's. When he gets back to the soda fountain, Derek's head is still tipped down, a hand rubbing his eyes.

"Derek," Harry says from the other side of the counter. "You don't want to be home? With your family? Your wife? Have a hot coffee, then I'll give you a lift."

"Home?" Derek looks up at Harry. His eyes are red-rimmed; his face, gaunt. "My wife's there now. Her parents drove up from Pennsylvania. But I can't go back home. All I see there is Abby. Everywhere I look." He stops, shakes his head. "Her backpack on the floor. Her drawings on the fridge. Her stuffed animals. Her snacks." He takes a long breath. "Abby has this horse stable thing. A play set. It's got this wooden stable box filled with

60

different horses." Quiet, then, "An Appaloosa. A painted pony." Another breath. Then? Nothing.

Harry comes around the counter and sits on a stool beside his friend. Derek's a little older than he is, in his early thirties. And he seems really cold, or ... something. Harry looks down at the hem of Derek's jeans. Yes, they're still damp. Of course, they're wet with cove water. Derek must've wanted to dive in himself to find his little girl. Harry's sure someone had to have held him back.

"Derek," Harry says. "Where's your coat, man? You must be freezing."

"My coat."

"Yeah."

"My coat." Derek shoves up his flannel shirtsleeve and checks his watch. He does this thing, too, where he just breathes. When he finally does talk, his voice is low, monotone. "Hours ago, I got a call at work to get to the cove, right away. So I went, you know? To the cove."

"Sure," Harry says, nodding.

"When I got there, all I saw were flashing lights. Roadblocks on the street. Ambulances, paramedics, fire trucks. Everything was blocking me from Abby. I had to get through."

"My God, Derek."

"And I finally saw them. Men wearing yellow dive suits. I saw them bring up my daughter's body from beneath the water. Saw her limp arms as they ran to shore holding her. I watched them do chest compressions ... and try to breathe life back into her."

Harry hears Derek form each word. Hears how dry his mouth is. Derek's got nothing left. No emotion. No tears.

61

No spit, even. Barely a breath—those come with effort, as though he has to remind himself.

"You know something, Harry? Their attempts to save her were heroic, but almost violent, in a way. Desperate. And that's how I knew." Derek forces some painful swallow past a sudden lump in his throat. "She was just gone."

"Hang on," Harry says, clasping Derek's arm as he gets up. "Wait right there."

Because suddenly Harry knows. He appreciates something his father did. Or rather, something his father kept. His father never said a word about it, but Harry understands now. He runs to the back room and grabs the bottle of whiskey from a dusty shelf there. Sometimes, when someone's hit bottom, that's all there is. He brings the whiskey to the soda fountain, grabs a couple of glasses and fills each. When he slides one in front of Derek, he takes a long swallow.

"She was so drenched, Harry. Her hair, it was … dripping. Her clothes, heavy with water. Water, everywhere. Freezing water. So when they laid her on the cold stretcher, I had to do it. Do something. I tried to get off my coat as I ran over. My arm, it got twisted up in it and … I panicked. I thought I wouldn't be able to get it off for Abby."

"For Abby?"

"It wasn't right, Harry. She was so cold." Derek takes another sip of the liquor. He doesn't really look at Harry when he talks, though. It's obvious that all he sees is the tragic scene at the cove. "That's where my coat is. She needed my warm coat over her. So I finally yanked it off and—"

That's it. He just stops talking, as though he's done.

Harry sits silently on a stool beside him and takes a sip from his own whiskey. A minute passes like that in the store, everything still. An occasional car drives by outside. The radiators tick with rising warmth. Until Derek gets his head together and continues, his words coming slowly, with care.

"I laid my coat over her body," he whispers so quietly, Harry scarcely hears him. "Pressed it to her sides. But gently, Harry. Gently. In case she was in any pain. I knelt down and tucked it all around her on the stretcher. When I was done? I set my hand on her face, touched her sopping hair. But it was her face, well, I thought if I stroked it, if I could press some life back into it, and I tried but … So I hugged her. Right there beside the cove, my daughter not moving on that stretcher. And I told her how much I loved her." Derek lifts his chin then, in a defiant way—as though he's telling the gods, or fate, or luck that he *won't* back down from what they just dealt him.

"Oh man, Derek," Harry barely says.

And he sees it, that restraint Derek employs. That defiance against the world crashing in on him today. Harry watches as Derek lifts his empty whiskey glass and thumps it on the countertop, over and over. Each thump angrier and angrier, as though he wants to take that glass and heave it across the room. Fling it crashing into a window, or wall, or some random display of ornaments.

Derek doesn't, though. Instead, he reaches over for the whiskey bottle and fills his glass again.

"I'm so sorry, Derek."

Silence, a sip of liquor, then, "Me, too. The other kids?

63

They said they were walking home from school and wanted to go skating this weekend. Said Abby took a few steps on the cove to test the ice. That the ice broke when she turned around to come back. It just made a snapping sound—one snap—and she was gone. Seven years old, Harry, my Abby was. That's all I got, seven years with her."

Harry sits there, silently. In a few moments, he walks over to the store's sweatshirt display. Each one—hoodies and pullovers and zip-ups—is screen-printed with the Dane's General Store logo. He rummages through a folded pile and picks a large fleece-lined zip-up. It's all he can do, really. When he walks back with it, Derek takes it. He manages to get his arms in the sleeves, then pulls the fabric up around his neck. His overgrown dark hair brushes the collar; his eyes are empty; his fatigue, bleak.

Later, much later, after Harry closes up the store and drives Derek home, he heads home, too. It's unfathomable to him how anyone, how Derek, can walk into a house so familiar, so completely your own, and have it be utterly ruptured. In Derek's life, that cove swallowed everything—it was written all over him tonight.

Harry sits alone in the tufted armchair in the living room now. His parents are asleep; the house is quiet. The whole town went quiet today, a part of everyone lost in that one drowning.

But still, Harry takes a lesson from Derek. He raises his chin in defiance of the evil that lurks in places unknown. Yes, he turns on a table lamp near the chair, and the Christmas tree lights, too. The lights cast a soft glow on the stuffed snowman sitting on the fireplace hearth, on the garland strung from the mantel. Some Christmas cards are stacked on the coffee table, so Harry grabs those and sits again. Holding the cards in his lap, he first just looks at the twinkling tree. The room is silent. In a moment, he opens one card, then another. There are greetings from near and far, the usual warm wishes and good cheer penned in personal notes in so many of them.

But one in particular moves him tonight. He reads it once, then again.

> *Merry Christmas from my first apartment! Main Street Keene is twinkling with decorations. Here in New Hampshire, the holidays have arrived ... Hope you have a good one, Lorrie.*
>
> *Warmly,*
> *Sadie*

So the world keeps turning, no matter what. Shocking tragedies have got nothing on it. Maybe they can't. Life goes on, and on; there's no stopping it.

Well. The world turns for some. For others—defiant or not, strong or not—it stops. Stops right on its axis and may not ever start up again.

Derek Cooper's world stopped spinning today. Stopped cold, the moment he laid his warm coat over his unmoving daughter.

ten

The Tenth Winter

THE JAM WENT EVERYWHERE. WILD strawberry jam, and peach jam, and apple-cider jelly, and blackberry seedless. From Concord grape to beach plum, a veritable smorgasbord of local, hand-stirred, bottled jams covers everything in the store.

Or … everything within reach of impact.

"We're in a jam, Pop," Harry says from the phone in the back of the store.

"What? What are you talking about?"

Harry looks at his fingers stickied with jam from moving some of the debris, then looks up at the gaping hole in the roof. "We're in a jam. *Literally.* I was outside the store shoveling snow and heard a loud bang. When I went inside to check it out, part of the roof had caved in! Right on top of the jam display."

"What? Are you okay? You didn't get hurt, did you?"

"No. No, I'm good. Was outside when it gave out.

Luckily, I hadn't opened the store yet, so no customers were inside either. But what a mess, let me tell you. There's jam everywhere!"

"That old roof must've collapsed beneath the weight of all the snow. How bad is it?"

"Well." Harry ventures a few steps further into the general store. He walks past the still-intact glass case holding knit scarves and fleece-lined gloves. Beyond the case, though, shards of rafters hang; wet ceiling plaster sags; roof shingles dot the floor; chunks of snow grow purple and red from the spilled jam; snowflakes spin down from a visible patch of sky. "Not *too* bad. It's a small part of the roof. But the rest of it should be inspected now, to be sure the structure is sound."

"All right, good idea. Don't need anything else coming down—walls, more roof. I know a guy, I'll give him a call from here at home, then meet you there."

So Dane's General Store loses a day of business, two weeks before Christmas. That's all it takes—one day—for engineers to analyze the damage and for a local contractor to have his crew temporarily repair the roof, safely patching and shoring it up so the store can reopen tomorrow. Electricity was shut off, too, until all wiring and gas lines were confirmed unharmed. His mother briefly stopped by with her movie camera to film the damage: the jagged opening in the roof; the snow falling through it right onto the floor; the jam. It helped that Emma came by later, too. Together, Harry, his father and sister got the store tidied up, everything shipshape.

"We did the best we could salvaging most of the inventory," Harry tells his mother when he and his father arrive home that evening. "But all the jam's a total loss."

Norm hands Linda a box. "The new dishtowels even got soiled. That jam splattered everywhere. Triple berry went this way, strawberry rhubarb, that."

"Oh! Those pretty flour sack towels I just put on display?" Linda brushes through the box of colorful towels printed with roosters and red apples and sprigs of herbs. "I'll get them cleaned up nicely, good to go." When Harry's mother sets the box on the kitchen counter, she brushes off her tacky fingers.

"See?" Harry asks while pulling off his snow-dusted hat. "Jam. Everywhere. Even on the box."

"Emma helped rearrange Bea's Brownies and bags of Christmas gumdrops to fill in the empty jam display. Oh, and she's coming for dinner, too," Norm says while setting aside his snowy gloves. "Bringing her new boyfriend, Garrett. Wants us to meet him."

"Well, I wish she'd told me that!" Linda motions to a large pot simmering on the stove. "I would've cooked something fancier than beef stew."

"Don't sweat it, Ma." Spoon in hand, Harry ventures closer to the stove for a taste of that stew. "Emma says Garrett's real down-to-earth."

"Ah, it's good to finally be home anyway," Norm says while Harry's mother helps him off with his coat. He hangs it on a hook near the back door. "Be needing a new roof on that store, Linda. Soon as the weather warms in the spring. It's just patched for now."

"That's a big job, Norm." Linda sets two more dishes

on the table, then swats Harry away from the stove and gives the stew a stir.

"Got to be done, though." Norm's washing his hands at the sink, soaping off any jam remnants.

"Hey, Pop," Harry says, sitting at the farm table and unlacing his boots. "Maybe you can kill two birds with one stone. You mentioned someday renovating the barn behind the store. Clean it up some, get more storage out of it."

"Now that's an idea, son. Have all that construction work done at once?"

"You could. If it doesn't set you back too much." Harry drops his boots near the back door and grabs up a pile of envelopes from the counter there. "Brought the mail in for you, Ma. Where do you want it?"

Linda glances over from the stove. "Put it in the living room, would you? I'll look at it later." As Harry crosses the kitchen, she calls out, "Dinner in ten minutes!"

Ten minutes. That's the longest Harry's had to sit and rest all day. Between talking to the roofing crew, and picking up the debris, and sweeping up broken jam-jar glass, and wiping jam from shelves and displays—then washing down the floor and surrounding area, not to mention showing around the electric company techs and turning away customers at the door—it's been a long day. Cold, too, with no heat in the store until they got the okay to switch it back on later.

So he sits in the tufted armchair beside the fireplace and idly thumbs through the mail. Ten minutes until dinner? Harry's so tired, he could sneak in a catnap for those minutes. Maybe he'll do just that after opening the

Christmas cards that arrived. First, he shoulders off his cargo jacket and folds it over the chairback. There are only three cards today, but it's the third that has him get up from his seat and return to the kitchen while reading it.

> *Season's Greetings, Lorrie. Office party tonight. I've got a dapper date, who happens to be my coworker Rex. Oh! There's the doorbell.*

> *Till next year,*
> *Sadie*

"Ma," Harry says a moment later as he leans in the kitchen doorway. His mother's scooping steaming beef stew into a serving bowl while his father slices hunks of Italian bread. "Didn't you ever send this Sadie person a note?"

"Did we get another card from her?"

"Sure did." Harry looks down at the card. On it is an illustration of Santa and his reindeer flying over a snowy winter wonderland. "She must think those people you bought the house from still live here."

"I swear I sent that Sadie a note last year. Or was it two years ago?"

"Maybe. Or maybe not. But you should, to let her know her friends don't live here anymore. Because you've got a whole drawer full of cards from her in the other room." Harry holds out this year's Santa card, and when his mother takes it from him, she gives an extra tug when it sticks to a jam-sticky spot on his fingers.

eleven

The Eleventh Winter

SIGN HERE. AND HERE," THE mortgage loan officer says. She flips a page over. "Here, too. On the bottom."

Harry does, writing his name on every dotted line, every solid line, every outlined signature box—top, bottom, left and right, over and over again.

"Initial and date, there." The mortgage rep slides another formidable-looking, multipage document across the table to him. "Two times, then again on the second copy."

When his ink fades, Harry gives his pen a good shake and tries again. Signatures, initials, dates—never has a moment felt so significant.

"A few more," his lawyer says then. He opens a legal-sized folder and brushes through documents, forms, transfers, declarations, disclosures. "Here. And there." For each form Harry signs and sets aside, another two follow. "Signature on the bottom, twice. Initial the back."

Words are serious, too. *Form of ownership—individual.* And *Bill of sale—personal property being transferred.* The words get more formal. *Notarized affidavit of title. Down payment. Gift of equity.* And then come the words that have Harry sweat, *Amount of debt. Term of loan. Payment schedule. Mortgagor.*

Finally, after the last of the i's are dotted and t's crossed, it happens. His father reaches across the conference room table and hands him a keychain with a shiny new key to the Craftsman bungalow. "It's all yours now, son. Congratulations!"

"But I already have the keys, Pop. I've lived there since after college."

"It's a ceremonial thing, Harry," his mother says. Her eyes well up as she stands and gives him a hug. "We're very proud of you. Twenty-eight years old and buying your first house."

"Thanks, Ma. And remember. Christmas is at *my* place this year."

‌

Now that's something Harry never imagined saying anytime soon. *Christmas at my place.*

But if there's one thing he's learned recently, it's that some things you never do see coming. This real estate closing? It culminates a *year's* worth of those moments, starting with the general store's roof repair.

Which expanded into a full renovation of the storage barn behind the store. A barn redesigned mostly into a barn *apartment*, with some storage space left intact in the rear.

And during all that construction chaos of walls coming down and drywall being installed and light fixtures being hung, something else happened that no one saw coming: His sister, Emma, secretly eloped with Garrett. *Surprise!*

Which resulted in unexpected parties and dinner celebrations toasting the newlyweds.

Followed by Harry's parents also doing something no one ever saw coming. They decided to downsize and move *into* that utterly charming barn apartment. "It's so close to work, Harry," his father told him one recent November morning. The two of them were having coffee at the soda fountain before the store opened for the day. "All I have to do is walk across the parking lot."

"But what about the house?" Harry asked. "You love that Craftsman, Pop."

"Well, son. We were wondering if you'd like to buy it."

The answer to which, yes, Harry *never* saw coming.

An answer that led to today's real estate closing.

Harry thinks all this as he drives the Addison country roads now, crosses the covered bridge and finally turns onto Birch Lane, to his very first home. He pulls in the driveway, parks the car, sits there and looks through the windshield at the house he owns. *His* house.

His olive-green Craftsman bungalow that he'd once believed could *never* feel like home. Has it already been a decade since he drove here for winter break during his freshman year of college? He'd sat in his car in this very same driveway. Looked out at the clapboard siding, and shingled second-story front dormer, and large stone chimney of the house his parents had just bought. Has it been ten years since that day, when his father first rushed out the front door and down these same porch steps to greet him?

Now this *is* his home. Every shingle, window and door. The house whose lawn he'll mow, whose walkway he'll shovel. The house whose living room walls he'll change to a fresh taupe. Whose porch swing he'll recushion. Whose planked front door he'll paint a rustic white. The house whose property taxes he'll pay. The house for which he'll make a mortgage payment every month for the next thirty years.

Home.

He gets out of the car, checks the mailbox and walks up the sidewalk to the bungalow's front porch.

Home, sweet home.

Inside, it's quiet. And all his.

Harry sets his real estate documents on the kitchen counter and thumbs through the mail before he'll head over to the store for the afternoon. A few Christmas cards are mixed in with the bills and catalogs that came. One card is for his parents—from someone who must not be aware that they moved. Another card is for Harry. And the last? That one, well, that one's for Lorrie and Allan.

"Ah, yes. Sadie." Standing in his kitchen, Harry opens her envelope and pulls out the card. It's a painting of a single ornament set on sprigs of evergreen. The red glass ball is etched with pale gold leaves, and a thin red ribbon loops around and around the ornament's cap. Harry opens the card and reads the message written across the bottom.

Off to a winter wedding this weekend—not mine, though! Not yet, anyway … Rex and I are doing fine. I think you'd like him, Lorrie.

Christmas Cheers from Sadie

"Sadie, Sadie," Harry whispers. He goes to the living room to see if his mother emptied out the Queen Anne end table before she moved to the barn apartment. When he opens the drawer, at least ten cards are there. Harry brushes his hand over some—crisscrossed candy canes; red cardinals on a fence post; a prancing reindeer. He looks at the ornament card in his hand and adds it to the pile of cards from this mysterious Sadie.

Sadie Welles, to whom his mother always meant to send a little note, explaining that Lorrie and Allan had moved away.

"Guess it's up to me now," Harry says before closing the drawer and getting himself to the general store for the afternoon shift.

twelve

The Twelfth Winter

IT'S HAPPENING, FOR THE FIRST time ever. Happening at the Dane's General Store tent at the Coveside Cornucopia Festival.

"We're sold out, Pop," Harry says. Behind him, the tent shelves are empty.

"Sold out?" His father gives change to a customer at the cash drawer. "Of T-shirts?" he asks, looking over his shoulder at Harry.

"Of *everything*," Harry tells him. "It's all gone—tees, sweatshirts, hats. Even the coffee mugs."

"Now that's a first. Sold out!"

"Completely. Why don't you go back to the store to get more inventory? I'll man the tent while you're gone."

And man the tent, Harry does. A steady stream of people—young and old, families, couples and singles—drifts to the store's tent at Coveside Cornucopia. Beyond them, Addison Cove glistens beneath a November-blue sky. Harry can just imagine how hundreds of years ago, this very cove was a shipping port for sea trade from the West Indies and British colonies. Coveside Cornucopia celebrates that with food trucks, arts and crafts, and a few boats bobbing on the water. Billowing sails are rigged on their decks, making them look historical. Except instead of trading the grains, sugars, red onions and molasses of yore, the festival crowds are buying crafts, and local artwork, and … fudge?

Because that's where the people at the Dane's tent are coming from—the *Fran's Fudge* tent beside theirs.

When his father returns with a box of goods to restock, Harry walks over to that neighboring tent to see what all the fuss is about. He buys a piece of chocolate fudge. Then another. Which is when he also mentions that Dane's General might like to carry some in the store.

So he ends up with a business card from the woman who owns *Fran's Fudge*, along with an invitation to stop by their commercial kitchen a few towns over. There, he can sample more fudge flavors and choose which he'd like to order for the store.

"Excuse me," Harry calls out a week later when he walks into the busy professional fudge kitchen. A woman bent over a long marble tabletop motions for him to wait. Holding a partially wrapped stick of butter, she's using both hands to push and pull the butter, back and forth, over the entire table. When she's done and approaches him, a young fudge cook spreads peanut butter over that entire buttered surface. Beyond, immense copper pots are simmering over burners. A man uses a long wooden spoon to stir some liquid chocolate mixture in one of the pots.

"Hi there," the woman says, wiping her hands with a towel as she heads Harry's way. Looking to be about fifty, she wears a bib apron, with a bandana-like chefwrap on her head. "Can I help you?"

"I'm Harry. Harry Dane, from Dane's General Store," Harry tells her. "Met you at Coveside Cornucopia?"

"Oh, yes. Of course." She walks around another marble table. There, a cook uses a long-handled spatula to work a steaming fudge mixture back and forth across the tabletop.

Harry holds up the business card she'd given him. "I'm here to sample flavors we'd like to stock," he says, glancing quickly at the card. "Fran?"

She nods and points to a room behind him. "Can you wait in there? Just be a minute."

Giving another glance at the fudge operation happening on buttered marble-top tables and in steaming pots, Harry heads over to the room. It appears to be a small conference room walled with windows looking out onto the fudge-making operation. Harry sits at the long table there and waits. A few minutes later, the swinging door opens and a woman backs into the room while holding a loaded tray in her arms.

"Harry?" the woman asks, setting the tray of fudge samples on the table. She's tall and slender, and also wears an apron over her jeans and long-sleeved tee. "I'm Fran."

"Fran?" Harry looks toward the kitchen where he

spoke with the other woman. "But I thought—"

"That's my mom. Louise." Fran nods to her mother out at the fudge tables. "I'm her daughter, Francesca."

"Fran." Harry stands and shakes her hand.

"Yes," she says, giving a shrug and small smile. "Mom named the business after me." Fran pulls out a chair, sits and motions for him to sit again, too. "I understand you want to carry our fudge in the general store?"

When Harry sits across from her, Fran right away sets out fudge samples on several paper plates.

Fran, with dark brown hair, her bangs sweeping across her hazel eyes.

Fran, whose confident hands point out different flavors: *chocolate peanut butter*, and *chocolate sea-salt caramel*, and *white-chocolate cranberry*, and *maple walnut*.

Fran, whose eyes sparkle every time that wide smile fills her face.

Fran, whose soft voice is as sweet as every fudge sample Harry tastes.

All our fudge is made by hand.

Custom flavors.

Family-run business.

Mail order and local.

Fran, whose name Harry doesn't say again until after he places an order for the general store and stands to leave. Then, well then he says her name only once more, before walking out the door.

"Listen, Fran. It was really nice talking to you. And, I don't know." He stops as he lifts his cargo jacket off another chair. "I was thinking we could maybe …" As if reading his mind, she slightly nods, while her sparkling eyes watch him—which makes him clear his throat. And put on his coat. "If you're not busy, I mean … We could get a coffee sometime?"

When she tells him that right now's a good time, Harry thinks the day couldn't get any sweeter.

∾

Fran. Harry says her name often, then, throughout the Christmas season. Tells people about Fran, and how they're seeing each other.

To his friend Greg Davis: *Going to the tree-lighting, with Fran.*

To his mother, when she's working the register at Dane's on a day when Fran stops by: *Ma, this is Francesca. Fran.*

To Nate, when he asks Harry if he's bringing anyone to his holiday house party: *Fran. You'll get to meet Fran.*

To his father: *Pop, What should I buy Fran for Christmas? Got any good ideas?*

To everyone at the Small Business Christmas Party at the boathouse: *This is Fran.* Or, *I'd like you to meet Fran.*

To his sister: *Finally got myself a girl, Emma. Fran.*

But mostly, Harry says her name to Fran, herself. On the phone; before he leans in and kisses her; when he picks her up for a ride through town on the Holly Trolley; after they build a snowman together; in bed, when he wakes up beside her and touches her hair on snowy December mornings; when he brings in his mail one day close to Christmas.

"Fran," he calls to her in the kitchen, where she's

making a pot of spaghetti. "Come here for a minute."

While he waits, he sits in the tufted armchair beside the stone fireplace. Boxes of ornaments are stacked on the hearth so that they can decorate his tree together this evening. He holds an envelope in his hand and raises it up when Fran walks into the living room.

"What is it, Harry?" she asks, then sits on the arm of the chair and touches his shirt collar, his jaw. "Everything okay?"

"I just want to tell you a story," he says.

And he does. He shares the story of Sadie Welles, and how she's been sending cards to this house for twelve years now, unaware that the previous owners have left. He explains how his mother was going to get in touch a few times, but life got in the way, then the years went by, and the cards were set aside.

"Here." Harry gives her Sadie's unopened envelope. "You read this year's card."

"Ooh, I don't know," Fran says. "Maybe you should just write *Return to Sender* on the envelope."

"What's another year at this point?" Harry asks. "She's got to put things together, eventually."

So Fran does it. Carefully, she tears open the envelope and pulls out a card. Berries and sprigs of greens spill from the tops of two white ice skates hung on a red door.

"What's it say?" Harry asks. "Sadie's note."

Fran looks at him, then opens the card. "*Dear Lorrie,*" she begins. "*Changes this Christmas. The advertising agency I've been with since my college internship is closing its doors. Not sure what's next. Hope you and Allan are well.*" Fran looks at the ice skate image again, then gives the card back to Harry. "*Fondly, Sadie,* she writes."

Harry opens the card and sees Sadie's familiar cursive sweeping across the bottom of the card, like always. He runs his finger across the words.

"Don't you think maybe *you* should let her know those people moved away?" Fran softly asks. "Since she's still mailing their card here?"

"Not sure. After all this time ..."

"Oh! That's the pasta! Come on." Fran leans down and kisses Harry's cheek when a timer beeps in the kitchen. "Dinner's about ready."

"Be there in a sec," he says as Fran rushes back to the stove. Standing, Harry walks to the paned windows and looks out on the evening. Up and down Birch Lane, colorful lights are strung over shrubs; garland loops across a white picket fence; a wreath hangs on a massive front-facing chimney on the Tudor across the street; snow gently falls beneath coach-light lampposts.

When Harry hears Fran setting out dishes and silverware, he looks at Sadie's card, then puts it with the others in the Queen Anne end table drawer. It's a little surprising how many cards have accumulated there—snowmen and Santas and wintry woodland scenes and decorated front doors—with little notes in each. He pauses for a long second, then closes the drawer and joins Fran in the kitchen for dinner, just as she sets a plate of warm rolls on the table.

thirteen

The Thirteenth Winter

THEIR WORDS ARE FEW. AND Harry's heart? Heavy.

When Fran moved in with him early summer, it was just the opposite. Birds were singing; the hydrangeas blossomed in his yard; skies were blue; Harry whistled with each carton he hauled from Fran's car to his house. He was in love, and thought that by Christmas he and Fran might be engaged.

Never thought that the same boxes and totes he carried up the walkway, across the front porch and past the painted entrance door to his Craftsman bungalow would soon be leaving. Soon be packed and taped and carried in the reverse direction—out of the bedroom, down the hall, across the living room, out the front door, down the porch steps to Fran's car. Its doors and trunk are open now; the backseat already stacked high with her things.

Even worse? They hardly speak.

There's just not much to say, this time. And he gets it.

Most of their words were already said after Fran attended the Future of Fine Chocolate Conference. Her unexpected words told Harry there was someone else. She'd met a chocolatier. And they had so much in common, including plans for her fudge business. And, well, *this* wasn't going to work.

"This?" Harry asked.

"Us," Fran softly said, her smile small, her eyes damp.

So today, as her belongings leave his house beneath a gray December sky, Harry feels disappointment more than anything else. His desperate words trying to convince her to stay, her sad words turning him down, had all been said, uttered, pleaded, whispered. Been spent. As had their emotions.

Now, they're just getting through the morning before he heads to the store for his afternoon shift.

"Where do you want this box?" Harry asks as he's going down the porch steps and Fran's coming up.

"Oh, that one has my laptop in it. Can you put it on the front seat?"

And so it goes, back and forth. It's actually pretty incredible how many things one person brought into his house in only a few months: clothing and dishes and shoes and framed photographs and linens and small pieces of furniture. The list goes on as they pass each other again and again—he in one direction, she in the other—carton-laden arms brushing, *Oops, sorry,* murmured. Coming in, going out, stepping aside, holding the door.

"Your jewelry box is in this one." Harry nods to the plastic tote in his arms as he goes out the front door and

Fran approaches the porch. "Is there room in your trunk?"

"Yes." Fran takes the tote from him. "I'll put it in next to my stepstool."

When she crosses the front lawn to her car, Harry watches before going inside again for the last few things. When he heads back outside, carrying an armload of clothes-on-hangers through the front door, Fran's coming up the walkway. A stack of envelopes and flyers are in her hands, so Harry stops there on the porch. He stands against the open wood-planked door.

"Mail came," Fran says, thumbing through the envelopes before looking up at him.

"Anything of yours you need to take when you leave?"

She shakes her head. "No. Just a catalog I'd like. Oh," she says then. "Wait." She pulls out a green envelope. "Looks like there's a Christmas card from that lady you told me about. The one who sends a card for someone else every year?"

"Sadie."

Fran glances at the return address. "It is." She shrugs and walks past him, into the house. "You'll forward any of my mail to me?" she asks over her shoulder.

"I will." With Fran's clothes draped across his arms, Harry heads down the porch steps.

"Well, what about this—" Fran's voice calls out as he's bent into her car's backseat and hanging her clothes on the hook there. He doesn't hear the rest.

A few minutes later, when Fran emerges from their bedroom, Harry's sitting at the kitchen farm table. It's been a long morning and he's beat. As Fran walks into the room, she's pulling a wool beanie onto her head.

"That's about it, Harry. I think I've got everything."

He nods. That's it, just nods.

"Harry." Fran stops in the doorway and turns toward him. "It wasn't anything you did. It's just that, well, things happened with me and—"

"Fran." He looks up at her. "We've covered it all already."

"Okay." She turns to leave, then stops and glances over her shoulder. "Take care, Harry."

He looks long at her. "You, too," he finally says.

And those words? They seem to free her. Keys in hand, Fran hurries through the house, goes out the front door and is gone. Just like that.

But in that one blur, it feels like she's taken the past few months with her. Taken the memories—tending their vegetable garden together, long summer walks, twilight dinners on the back patio.

Taken her smile; and her soft brown bangs brushing against her beautiful eyes; and her nighttime touch; her morning kisses.

All of it—gone.

That sudden empty feeling has Harry rush to the front door to see for himself. To see Fran leave right as her car backs onto the street and she drives herself and their memories down Birch Lane. He watches until the car is out of sight.

The house feels empty now. There's that hush again, one that he'd gotten used to before Fran moved in. Closing the door behind him, Harry decides to give the house another walk-through. He passes the copper pans hanging on the dining room wall. Turning into the living room, he stops and looks around at the braided rug on the wide-planked floor; at the white crown molding; at the coffee and end tables; at the built-in shelves near the stone fireplace. The kitchen comes next, where he scans the countertop and opens a few painted cabinets. Maybe Fran left behind a favorite coffee cup. Or a scarf. Her blue pen. A hairbrush. Something. *Anything* that might give him a reason to call her back.

But she made a clean sweep of the place and there's nothing left. So instead, Harry makes a sandwich: turkey, tomato and cheese on wheat bread. When the sandwich is heating in the microwave, he goes to throw out the deli wrapping from the last of the cheese.

Which is when he notices something. Something green, poking out from beneath a few crumpled papers in the wastebasket. It's an envelope. You could almost miss it, the way a store flyer and damp paper towel cover it. But that one corner of the envelope gives it away.

Harry brushes aside the trash and pulls out Sadie's card. So Fran tossed it—as if there's no point in reading someone's private thoughts not intended for them. Harry looks toward the door where Fran just left. Looks at the card again. Glances to the door once more, then gives the card a shake and presses a wrinkle out of it before slicing open the envelope with a knife. After pouring a glass of juice and getting his lunch plate from the microwave, he sits at the table. And bites into his sandwich.

Then, he does it. He takes out the holiday card. The picture on front is of a spindly pine tree in a wooded clearing. The tree's scrawny limbs are dusted with snow; a single red ornament hangs from a branch. Harry opens the card and finds Sadie's message this year.

Hello, Lorrie.

Remember when we planned the neighborhood pet show? Well, I'm back at my alma mater, doing event planning for the college now. After losing my advertising job last year, I ended up staying in New Hampshire, but Rex didn't … Sending warm Christmas wishes to you and Allan.

Sadie

Giving another look at the solitary tree image, Harry props the card on the table. "You and me both, Sadie," he says as he brings his lunch things to the sink and cleans up. "Dumped."

∽◌

Later, when Harry arrives at the general store, a local high school student is ringing out folks at the register.

"My father around?" Harry asks her.

"Over there." She points to the other side of the store. "At the bird feeders."

Harry walks over to a wall aisle, where his father is placing new inventory on a shelf. "Hey, Pop," Harry says as he lifts a gazebo-shaped bird feeder from a nearby box.

"Harry." His father takes the hand-carved feeder from him. "We need to stock up on birdseed. Folks are snatching these up for winter feeding."

"I'll get right on that. Place an order for you," Harry says as he heads to the back office.

"Gus Haynes was in earlier," his father adds. "Said black-oil sunflower seeds are good for the cardinals."

"Got it."

"Oh, Harry!" his father calls after him so that Harry turns back. "How'd it go today? You know, with Fran moving out."

Harry walks back toward his father. "It was a tough morning, getting her things packed up. For all these months, I really thought she might be the one."

"Well, we all liked Fran. I'm sorry things didn't work out, son."

"Yeah, Pop." Harry turns and heads to the office again. "Me, too."

fourteen

The Fourteenth Winter

YOU MAKING IT TO THE tree-lighting tonight, Norm?" a few customers ask at the register.

While Harry pours hot chocolate at the soda fountain counter, he eavesdrops on his father's conversation.

"Not this year. Manning the store here with my boy," Norm answers while making change.

"Too bad. Hear they got new lights for the tree. Energy-efficient LEDs this time. And they doubled up on the number of them."

"Should be something to see," Norm agrees while bagging hand-warmer packets. "Linda will be there with Emma and Garrett. They're bringing the new baby, too. It's Oliver's first Christmas."

"Shucks," the next woman in line says. "You're missing your grandbaby's first tree-lighting?"

"Oh, I'll see it, three times over! Linda's got her movie camera ready to capture the entire event for all of posterity. Wouldn't miss filming the moment that lil' guy first sits on Santa's lap."

As his father says it, his voice breaks, just a little. Harry can't miss it from where he's adding marshmallows to a hot cocoa, then sliding the cup to a customer waiting on a swivel stool.

Doesn't miss that wistfulness, again and again, as his father talks about tonight's tree-lighting to more customers buying mini flashlights and Bea's Brownies and thermal socks. Each time, Norm says a little more. Describes the cute red hat he bought for the baby. Tells how he and Linda babysat their grandson last weekend. *Have a portable crib set up in our barn apartment behind the store.* Mentions that the baby loved watching the birds at their window bird feeder—*Oh, how he'd smile!* And that they took him for a walk in the snow.

When Harry flips on the Christmas lights strung around the store's front porch, he looks out toward The Green. People are already gathering there. Food tents are arranged on the side; Santa's sleigh is set up beside the tree.

And that tree—it towers to the December sky, just a dark shadow in the dusky evening light right now, until the switch is thrown at nightfall.

"Why don't you take off, Pop?" Harry says when the store quiets down. "I've got things covered here."

"This is just a lull, son. Folks will be rushing in for last-minute things. Gloves, caps. It'll be mighty cold during that tree-lighting countdown."

Harry goes to the store's back room and lifts his father's coat and hat off the wall hook. "Tell you what.

You go," Harry says as he holds up his father's jacket. "Emma would want you there, with the baby and all."

"But what about you?" Norm asks as he slips into his jacket and zips it up.

"I've got a good view of that tree from here. I'll see it light up, especially with those new LED bulbs. Now go! I'll text Ma you're on your way."

"You sure?" Norm asks as he pulls on his hat.

"Listen, Pop. Just go and have a nice time. Take pictures of Oliver with Santa. And when the town tree's lit and everyone stops in here afterward to warm up, come back and help me serve cocoa at the counter."

"You're the best, Harry. You've got a deal!" his father calls over his shoulder as he rushes out toward The Green.

❦

Later, when Harry's giving the general store's checkerboard floor a quick sweep, he hears a vague chant. It's the annual countdown across the street, on The Green. Muffled voices are rising to the night sky. So he throws on his flannel-lined field coat and steps out on the porch to watch.

Seven! Six! Five! Four! Three! Two! One!

And … nothing.

No gloriously illuminated tree. Harry steps to the side and squints over at The Green. It's gone quiet, and the tree is still dark.

But soon after, a second countdown begins.

Five! Four! Three! Two! And one!

This time, instead of nothing, Harry *does* hear

something—a distant, collective groan. Still, no Christmas tree lights.

Wait a minute. That tree's supposed to have brand-new lights. So Harry figures something's got to be muddled with that change. Some wiring needs fiddling, some screw tightened, some defective string of lights replaced.

Well, if there's anything Harry's learned all these years managing the general store with his pop, it's this: how to tinker. Random folks always wander in looking for this size toggle bolt, or that size paint roller. They ask the best way to attach streamers to a child's bicycle handlebars, or if an egg slicer works on mushrooms. Some frazzled husband or young new homeowner is always wondering how to mend, repair, replace some sundry item in their homes.

Quickly, Harry throws a few electrical essentials into a toolbox in the back office. After grabbing his wool cap and locking up the store, he trots across the street to The Green. Families there are huddled together to keep warm while they wait. Working his way around the crowd, Harry joins a few men gathered in a fenced-off area behind the town's still-unlit tree. Their voices are low and serious as they shine flashlights on the electrical hookup. No surprise that his own father is there, scoping out the dark tree with the others.

"What's going on, Pop?" Harry asks as he nears. "Been waiting for that tree to light up."

"Harry." When his father sees the store's toolbox in Harry's hand, he nods. "These new LED lights? Their placement on the tree resulted in less cord reaching the outlet. The darn thing barely plugs in, son."

Harry walks closer and looks over the shoulders of several men. They stand behind the tree and fuss with the temporary electric panel wired and mounted there.

"That cord is just too short now, and pulls out of the outlet," one of the men explains to Harry. He points to the dark tree. "Looks like we'll have to restring some of the bulbs to accommodate the problem."

"Unless ..." his father says, turning to Harry. He squints at him as if he knows. As if, of course Harry is a master tinkerer—like father, like son—and knew exactly what to bring.

When Harry nods, snaps open his toolbox and pulls out a heavy-duty extension cord, a quiet cheer erupts among the men. The extension cord will suffice for tonight, until the lights can be adjusted in daylight tomorrow.

So this time, before the *third* countdown is initiated, the town leaders walk Harry Dane to the stage platform, where a ridiculously oversized, ceremonial light switch is mounted.

This time, after it's announced that Harry Dane saved Christmas for the town of Addison, Harry stands at the microphone to lead the chant.

This time, when the chant counts down, Harry gets the crowd cheering and whistling with anticipation between each uttered number.

Four! Three! Two! And ...

Before he says the last number, Harry reaches one gloved hand to that faux, oversized light switch. Putting his other hand to his ear, he prompts the crowd to call out the last number—*One!*—right as he flips the switch.

And right as he *prays* that his father is simultaneously coordinating the extension cord plug-in behind the tree.

It's a short prayer, because instantly, the grand town Christmas tree comes to life with thousands of lights twinkling like stars in the night. His pop came through for him, like he always does.

And if the town of Addison has any say in the matter, with that tree sparkling to the skies, all is suddenly right with the world.

⁓

After the tree-lighting, and after pouring countless cups of cocoa with his father at the store, Harry went home. He sits alone at his kitchen table now.

And he's still smiling at the thought of it all: that he saved Christmas.

While finishing up a late dinner, he reaches for the three-day stack of mail he's been too darn busy to open. A few Christmas cards are among the bills and department store catalogs. He opens the cards first. There are the familiar greetings from aunts and uncles—*See you on Christmas, Harry!* And the notes from old friends—*Photo is from our Bahamas cruise this year.* And, *Doing well. Hope you are, too.*

Finally? There's the card that has a way of surprising him each year—the one from Sadie Welles. He always forgets about her cards, until the next one arrives twelve months later. But the funny thing is how after all this time, her notes have become oddly familiar. It feels like he somehow knows her.

He pulls this year's card from the envelope. The illustration is of a grand red sleigh on gold runners. Wrapped and ribboned packages tucked this way and that spill from the sleigh's seat. And a harness of jingling bells is draped along the sleigh's edges. It's a happy card, giving the same sense of good holiday cheer that Harry felt at the tree-lighting earlier on The Green.

And when Harry opens the card, the happy celebration of this wintry Addison night seems to burst from *inside* Sadie's card, too. Sugary, shiny sprinkles fall from it, scattering over the farm table like pieces of tossed, glittery confetti.

Season's Greetings, Lorrie!

Took a Christmas cake-decorating class with friends tonight. Don't mind the powdered sugar and green sprinkles on the card.

Love to you and Allan,
Sadie

fifteen

The Fifteenth Winter

SOMETIMES THE SIGHT IS SO intimate, Harry has to look away.

"What's gotten into people?" he asks, nudging his father's arm at the register.

"People?" Norm asks back. "Like who?"

Harry hitches his head over to where Vera and Derek huddle together at the scented candle display. When Derek picks up a fat pillar, they lean in so close to sample its scent, you'd think they'd kissed. For each scent—vanilla, black cherry, caramel-apple spice, cinnamon—they touch, smile. Derek strokes a wisp of Vera's blonde hair. Vera squeezes his hand.

"It's the holidays, son. Brings out that spark in people."

When Wes Davis walks into Dane's General Store the next afternoon, he's not alone. Harry watches from behind the soda fountain as Wes never stops holding his new girlfriend's hand.

"Harry," Wes says when he and his girl each take a stool. "This is Jane. Jane March. We're, you know, seeing each other."

"Jane." Harry extends his hand across the counter.

"Nice to meet you, Harry," she says, shaking his hand. When she smiles, her expression is so genuine, the smile seems to reach right into her eyes.

"A couple of hot cocoas, Harry." Wes nods to a small pastry case on the counter. "And we'll split one of those apple-crumb bars."

Well. Split it, they do. Harry can't help but notice the way they lean in close. At one point, Wes even forks off a piece of the pastry and feeds it to this Jane. Jane, whose eyes never stop smiling at Wes.

"Harry, you ever try that speed-dating gig at the coffee shop?" Wes asks.

"At Whole Latte Life? Nah. Too busy this time of year."

"I get it, running the store and all." When Wes stands to leave, he takes Jane's hand again. "You should give it a go, though. Speed dating. Jane and I sort of stumbled into it a few months back."

Harry waves him off, and waves off the speed-dating thought, too. That's the last thing he wants to do at the end of a long day—swap tables and dates every three minutes, spilling the beans on his life story to one stranger after another. He glances outside at Wes and Jane crossing Main Street to The Green, right as Tom and Sara Beth Riley walk in.

Walk in and keep walking, straight to the assorted cheese selection where a sample tray is set out. Each cubed piece of cheese has a toothpick in it. When Tom and Sara Beth stop side by side and inhale the cheese scents, yes, they do it, too. They feed each other samples, deciding on which to buy.

"Just the cheese today," Tom tells Harry at the register. "Something nice to have with a glass of wine, you know?"

No, Harry doesn't know. Oh, he gets Tom's drift, though. A little wine and cheese on a snowy December night, maybe in front of the fireplace. Someone to snuggle with there, too.

It's the kind of night that's simply not in the cards for Harry Dane this year.

No, what's in the cards for Harry is just that—cards. Not toasting a beautiful woman by a roaring fireplace. Not clinking mugs of hot cocoa while settling in for a romantic Christmas movie, snowflakes tapping at the windowpanes.

Nope, instead he's got a stack of holiday cards from everyone *else* living that good life. Tonight, Harry brings a handful of those unopened cards to his living room, where garland loops across the rough-hewn mantel. His tree is lit; a meatloaf cooks in the oven; the shelf stereo plays. But when Sinatra starts crooning about mistletoe and holly, and stealing kisses, Harry looks over at the stereo speaker. "Sheesh. You, too, Frank?" he asks.

Shaking his head, Harry turns to his cards. There's one from his cousin, and another from his high school friend Steve and his wife, Pam. *Two kids now, Harry*, Pam wrote in the card. *A boy and a girl!* And from the empty nesters in the Tudor across the street? *Season's greetings, neighbor.*

And next, there it is—like clockwork. The annual Christmas card addressed to Lorrie and Allan. He taps the envelope on the arm of his chair. It's really hard to believe that this Sadie hasn't caught on that her friends have moved away. Sure, it doesn't help that Harry never let her know, but after all these years, what could he even say?

With that thought, he opens the envelope. Sadie's card shows a tolling gold bell nestled in a cluster of holly leaves and red berries. Harry opens the card, reads the verse, and sees the now-familiar cursive sweeping across the bottom of the card.

> *From my home to yours, Lorrie. It's my first Christmas at my very own condo. Been busy decorating. I hung a mirror over the fireplace, just like I remember you did, too.*
>
> *Warmly,*
> *Sadie*

Harry looks over at his fireplace—the very fireplace that Sadie's remembering. So she's been inside this house. On either side of the stone fireplace are built-in dark wood shelves, with small paned windows above them. But the mirror Sadie remembers? Long gone, now. At least, gone from here. Harry supposes it's hanging wherever Lorrie and Allan might live.

Maybe someday, Harry will send Sadie that little note after all. Just a few lines explaining things, letting her know how her cards mistakenly arrive here each year.

But not tonight.

Instead, Harry looks at her card again. Then he drops it in the end table drawer, walks to the kitchen and pulls the meatloaf out of the oven.

Harry's not sure why, but with each passing day, with each *ting-a-ling* of the bell over the general store's door, with each box of ornaments he rings out, with each hand-stitched pillow he stacks in a basket display, with each shovelful of snow he tosses off the walkway, he feels … glum.

Even as he switches on the twinkling lights wrapped around the general store's porch rails, that glumness doesn't go away.

The next week? Things in the store get even worse. Heck, Valentine's Day might as well be coming up, rather than Christmas. Especially with the way romance is blowing through town like a sudden snowstorm. Even his father has to smile and look away when George Carbone and his love, Amy Trewist, walk in. Because not only do they purchase a sprig of mistletoe, but, seriously? Does George really hold it over their heads so they can sneak a kiss right there in the home goods aisle?

Yes, there's no denying that this snowy holiday season, love is in the air.

Well, maybe the universe is trying to send Harry Dane a message. If the romantic odds are this good for everyone else this Christmas, maybe they're not half bad for him, either. So on his lunch break, Harry does it. Discreetly, in the confines of the general store's back room, he makes a phone call to the local coffee shop, Whole Latte Life.

"Um, hi," he says, clearing his throat. "I was wondering if you have any spots left for your next speed-dating night?"

sixteen

The Sixteenth Winter

HARRY CARRIES A BOX OF decorations in one arm, a take-out bag of fresh coffee cakes in the other. Though the sun is just coming up, there's a frosty chill in the air. Smoke curls from chimneys, and when he stopped at Snowflakes and Coffee Cakes? The bakery was crowded with folks rubbing their mittened hands together while waiting in line for warm, fresh-baked pastry.

From the general store's rear parking lot now, Harry sees a few lights on inside. Which isn't surprising, even at this early hour. His father is usually first to arrive, walking to the store from his barn apartment right behind it. Before flipping that *Closed* sign to *Open*, Pop likes to jump-start the day: percolate the coffee; wipe down counters; or at this time of year, put out Christmas decorations. That's his favorite. He changes it up, too: clusters of ornaments hanging from the ceiling one year; strings of lights crisscrossing that same ceiling the next. Often,

Harry's sister, Emma, helps line up nutcrackers on a shelf, or arranges a train set around their miniature snow village display in the front window.

But always, *always*, the general store—with its checkerboard floor and garland swags and tinsel and candy canes and gift-laden wood shelves—is simply magical by the time the decorating is complete. *Looks straight out of a Christmas storybook, Norm,* shoppers tell his father.

This morning, Harry shoulders open the rear entrance door and sets his things down on a table in the office there. He pulls off his wool cap, takes off his down-filled bomber jacket and hangs that over a chairback.

"Morning, Pop!" he calls into the store while checking for messages on his cell phone, then setting that down. "You want to pour us a cup of joe? I brought coffee cakes. Cinnamon crumb," Harry says as he opens the take-out bag and inhales the sweet aroma. "Got the ones made with whole-wheat flour and Greek yogurt, so they're good for you."

When his mother sends him a text message from the barn apartment, Harry texts back that they're about to take a coffee break before doing some decorating. Grabbing the pastry bag then, Harry walks out into the store. Only a few lights are on this early, but everything's clean as a whistle. The chrome stools at the soda fountain glimmer; the checkerboard floor shines. And the scent of fresh-brewed coffee fills the air.

"Smells great," Harry says, heading to the soda fountain counter. An undecorated three-foot-tall artificial tree is set on the end of it. Figuring his father's busy with something, Harry pours two steaming mugs of coffee. "I found that star you wanted for the tree," he goes on. "It was up in the attic at home. So I brought it." Turning, he sets the two mugs on the countertop and puts out napkins, too. "Pop? You're quiet today," he says, glancing out into the store.

Too quiet, Harry suddenly realizes. He steps out from behind the counter and looks across the store. All is still. Not even a sound of his father's footsteps, or of his tools tacking garland on the walls. Not a whistle, not a *Be right there, Harry*. Nothing.

So Harry walks further, past the tarnished copper trough filled with scented candles and locally made soaps.

Past the table covered with gift baskets, some filled with jams, others spilling with snow-dusted pinecones.

Past the canvas totes screen-printed with the Dane's General Store logo.

And he knows, when he first sees a thick piece of green garland on the floor. Something's wrong.

With another two steps, Harry sees more. Sees his father lying on the checkerboard floor in the paper goods aisle, beside the holiday display of snowflake plates and poinsettia cups. He's got on a cardigan sweater over his work pants, but he's not moving. He's on his back, with one foot splayed to the side. Packages of the holiday paper plates and cups are a mess around him on the floor.

"Pop!" Harry calls out, running over. Dropping to his knees, he turns his father's head toward him. His eyes open slightly; his face is pasty. "Pop, what happened? Are you okay?"

But, nothing. His father doesn't speak. He's breathing,

and looks at Harry. But his eyes are moist, and no words come. So Harry gives his shoulders a gentle shake. "Did you fall?" He looks over his shoulder for a ladder, or a stepstool his father might have been standing on. But neither is in sight. "Did you hit your head?"

When his father's eyes close, Harry leans lower. "No. No, Pop. You stay with me." He feels his father's face; the skin is damp with perspiration. Quickly Harry reaches into his pocket for his phone, but it's not there.

"*Shoot*," he whispers, looking over his shoulder toward the rear office, then at his father again. "I'll be *right* back. Right back. I'm just getting help. Don't worry."

Harry's not sure he's ever moved so fast—scrambling to the office, snatching up his cell phone and dialing 9-1-1. "I need an ambulance! *Now!* Yes, at Dane's General," he says while running back to where his father still lies on the checkerboard floor. Harry gives a few medical details into the phone, then, "Yes, he *is* breathing. *But hurry!*"

Kneeling beside his father again, this time Harry hears a wheezing sound. So he reaches over and loosens his father's shirt collar. "Help's on the way, Pop. Help's coming."

Never has a moment, a minute, a morning felt so urgent. When a distant sound of sirens gets closer, Harry glances back toward the store's entrance. The door's no doubt locked, so he runs over and unlocks it, then returns to his father. Taking his hand in his, Harry gives a squeeze. "You hang in there with me, Pop."

Harry Dane never made a promise he couldn't keep.

At least, not until now—two weeks after his father's funeral.

Two weeks after he watched his mother sit beside a hospital bed and whisper, *I love you, Norm.* Two weeks after his sister gave a tearful goodbye in that same hospital room, then looked back at Harry—arms crossed, silently watching—near the door.

Two weeks since Harry sat beside his father next, clasped one of Pop's hands in both his own and made a promise he now fears isn't in him to honor.

"I'll take care of things at the store," Harry said that early December morning in the hospital, his words serious. Everything was serious. His words. The equipment wired to his father to monitor his vital signs. The nurses, the doctor. The stark wall shelf near the window. His father's quiet struggle. "I'll get it decorated for Christmas, the way you like. Don't you worry, Pop, you hear me?" Harry looked closer at his father's sallow face. "You hear me? I'll keep the store running, just the way we always have, together. I already got the birdseed ordered. And an order of those all-natural soap bars came in."

Harry stopped then, and watched as his father didn't respond. As his slack face didn't move. But Harry felt it. Felt the slight squeeze of his hand that his father managed.

When a muffled sob came from his sister behind him, Harry looked over his shoulder at her, then quickly to his father again.

"I promise, Pop. I'll keep the store going—for you. *I promise*," Harry whispered before dropping his head and closing his eyes.

And he tried.

Lord knows, he tried. That garland his father held when Harry found him on the floor? The day after the funeral, that's the first thing Harry strung in a grand swag. And the countertop Christmas tree? Harry hung simple lights on it, and topped it with that tree topper he'd found in the attic. When his parents were newlyweds, his mother made that star-shaped topper from gold felt, outlined it in thin gold foil-garland and draped red and green ribbons from its base. After Harry set that felt star on top of the general store's tree, he stood a framed picture of his father on the counter beside it.

He hasn't been back to the store since.

Hasn't turned on the lights. Hasn't flipped the *Closed* sign to *Open*. Hasn't rung out holiday purchases at the register. Hasn't wished anyone a merry Christmas.

Sitting in his kitchen at home now, he finishes his dinner—some leftover chicken parm a neighbor had brought him after his father's funeral.

You have to eat, Harry, Pete Davis had said on the front porch when he handed him the wrapped dish the other morning. *You divvy this up and freeze the portions. Good hot meals will keep up your strength.*

After washing the dishes, Harry walks outside in the evening darkness to check his mail. It's been a few days since he's looked, so the mailbox is crammed. There are flyers, bills—and, yes—Christmas cards. Which are the last thing he'd expected this year. Walking up his porch steps, he sees the bare white-painted front door. There's been no decorating here at home. No wreath on the door; no Christmas tree near the fireplace; no garland on the mantel.

Just these cards now. So he sits at the kitchen farm table and opens them there. This year, the notes inside are different. Gone is the anticipation of a happy holiday. Gone are the smiles he used to almost feel in the messages. Instead, this year, his aunt writes, *Sending our love, Harry.* And a neighbor tells him, *Bess and I are thinking of you.*

The only card whose tone hasn't changed is Sadie's. Sadie Welles' card—with an old-fashioned red pickup truck on it. The truck is parked on a snowy lane. A wreath is mounted on its big silver bumper; a Christmas tree is propped in its bed. Harry looks at the image for several seconds, before finally opening the card to see what Sadie has to say.

> *It's Christmas in California this year! I've been dating my next-door neighbor at the condo. Visiting his family on the West Coast. Stay warm, Lorrie and Allan … We sure will!*
>
> *Merry Christmas from Sadie*

Harry sets the card with the others, stands up and looks around the kitchen.

And drags a hand through his hair.

And looks into the living room, where he turns on a table lamp and draws the curtains.

He stops then, and again looks around. Picks up the TV remote, sets it down.

Goes back into the kitchen, opens the fridge and takes a sip from a bottled water, then closes the fridge.

Finally, he does the same thing he's been doing these past few nights. He grabs his keys from the counter and heads out. Tonight, a light snow's begun falling. The flakes float in the beams of his pickup's headlights. It's a familiar route he drives. Could get there on autopilot. Driving through town, it's obvious Christmas is happening for everyone else. Grand trees light up living room windows. Waving mechanical Santas stand beside colonial lampposts. White birch deer adorn front porches. There are candles in paned windows; illuminated icicles dangling from roof overhangs; colored and white bulbs strung on picket fences.

The lights—they twinkle everywhere.

Everywhere except where he's headed.

Harry slows his truck as he drives around The Green, where the glimmering town tree towers to the sky. Huddled against the cold, a few families brave a wintry walk around the tree. But Harry keeps driving to Main Street. Storefronts are decked out in garland and ribbon; wreaths and lights. Shoppers hurry past in coats and hats; boots and mittens. With wrapped presents spilling from their bags, they rush in and out of tiny shops and boutiques.

Everywhere but at Dane's General Store.

Some well-meaning customer hung a wreath on the entrance door, but that's it. There are no tiny white lights outlining the storefront. No garland wrapped around the porch posts. The front windows are dark. The door locked up tight.

Since his father's funeral, Harry's often driven by the store, and kept right on driving. Then, the past few days?

110

He circled The Green once or twice while contemplating going into the store.

But in all this time since the day after the funeral, he hasn't.

Until now.

Harry pulls into the general store's driveway and parks around back. He goes in that rear entrance, hesitates, then closes the door behind him. Turning on an office light for some illumination, he walks further inside. The store is cold and damp; the space, shadowy. Hulking rows of shelves rise in the darkness. Like vague webs, vintage cooking utensils hang from rafters over the kitchen-supply row. Stacks of snow shovels stand like statues; garland—gold and silver—spills from dark wooden barrels.

Harry switches on the light over the soda fountain. Looking around, everything's the same—but it's different, too, without one man's presence. He didn't think it possible to miss someone as much as he misses his father. Without Pop walking in the back door from the barn apartment; or calling, *That you, Harry?* from the register; or unpacking a carton of goods over in paper products, Harry doesn't see the point of turning on all the lights. Of flipping the *Closed* sign to *Open*. Of arranging gift baskets or adding frothy whipped cream to hot cocoa or ripping a sheet of wrapping paper from the wall-mounted rolls of giftwrap.

Doesn't see the point of keeping the business going without Pop here. Without Pop opening up early; getting the coffee brewing; telling Harry what to order, what boxes to unpack; asking Harry about the house or a recent date or a new restaurant he tried.

Harry walks around the counter and sits on a swivel stool. That light over the soda fountain? It shines on the countertop Christmas tree, the one with a framed photo of his father beside it. In the picture, Pop stands in front of the general store on that long-ago day when they hung the new sign on the roof. He wears corduroy pants and a brown, thermal-lined jacket. And he couldn't appear happier. Looking at his proud father, Harry knows the point of keeping the store open—though he doesn't want to admit it.

The point is a promise he made to an honorable man. *I'll keep the store going for you, Pop. I promise.*

In the shadows, Harry walks through the store to the front windows. There is only the sound of his hiking boots on the checkerboard floor. Outside, snow is falling a little steadier. A young couple walks up the porch steps and approaches the entrance door. Maybe they see the dim light on over the soda fountain counter. Maybe they're just hoping to buy some stocking stuffer or ornament for the holiday. The man pulls on the door handle, but it's locked, of course. Harry steps aside, further into shadow, as the woman cups her eyes and tries to see inside the front windows before they move on.

How many times a day does that happen, Harry wonders. How many shoppers pass the store with a wistful glance, a sad smile? How many times does someone try the door, maybe give a knock or two?

In a moment, Harry walks to the back office and grabs that bottle of whiskey his father kept on a shelf there. He brings it to the soda fountain and pours a splash of the liquor into a glass. Before sitting on a swivel stool, he plugs in the tabletop Christmas tree, then shuts off the soda fountain light. The tree twinkles in the dark store, casting the faintest glow. That pale illumination reaches the homemade jam display. And the big basket of throw pillows that have catchy phrases stitched across them.

Harry walks around the counter and sits on a swivel stool near the tree. The tinsel-edged, gold felt star glimmers atop it. In the misty glow of the tree's lights, he can almost hear echoes of his father's voice. *Harry, give me a hand with this.* Or, *Harry, what do you think of hosting small events at the soda fountain? An engagement party. A birthday.* Or, *Let's just have a Kittens-for-Christmas sale.* Or, *We all liked Fran.* Or, *That jam splattered everywhere, didn't it, Harry?*

Memories, visions. This evening, they float like ghosts in the old general store.

Finally, Harry does it. Looking at his father's photograph, he raises his whiskey glass and swirls the amber liquor in it.

"I couldn't do it, Pop. Couldn't open the store. Not today." Harry downs his shot of whiskey. "But for you," he says, pulling the framed photograph closer, "I'll try again tomorrow."

seventeen

The Seventeenth Winter

DEAR LORRIE AND ALLAN,

Staying in and watching Christmas movies this snowy night. Fluffy slippers on, fresh-cut tree twinkling in the living room. Remember our movie nights all those years ago, Lorrie?

Missing you,
Sadie

If there's anything Harry Dane knows all about, especially in the year since his father died, it's missing someone. If he had to define it, he'd say that missing someone feels like a hole. A great big hole in his life that nothing can fill. Not a hobby. Not a dinner out. Not running laps. Not even being busy.

Which he is today. Busy as ever.

After a quick glance at his watch, he finishes his breakfast toast, downs his coffee and looks at Sadie's most recent card once more. On it, glittery red ornaments and green holly leaves spill from a white basket, all of it entwined in a loopy red ribbon. But it's her words about missing someone that stay with Harry as he drops her card in the drawer with the others and hurries off to work.

Because today's the day.

Harry went all out this December. He started decorating Dane's General Store right after Thanksgiving and didn't quit until he knew his father would be proud.

And today? Today he'll find out if he succeeded.

If he won Addison's annual Window Wonderland competition, in which the local Main Street shops, restaurants and businesses go all out with wintry window displays. Each year, Cooper Hardware or Wedding Wishes Bridal Boutique or Whole Latte Life Coffee Shop or Joel's Bar and Grille or Suitcase Escapes Travel Agency or even Luigi's Pizza has taken the prize. Dane's has never been declared the winning window, try as he and his father might.

But Harry feels it ... a change in the winter air. So maybe, just maybe, the swags of garland wrapped around the general store's porch posts and looped from the porch overhang will do the trick. This year, he wove a red-gingham ribbon through the garland, along with the white lights.

Or will the outdoor Christmas tree secure the win? A decorated four-foot tree stands in a banded wooden barrel on the other side of the porch, beside the double windows. Windows behind which a model train chugs 'round and 'round a snow village set out in tufts of white cotton. A village in which a ceramic steepled chapel and toy store and post office and snow-laden gingerbread cottages sit among bottle-brush trees and clusters of singing caroler figurines, their heads tipped up to the skies. Fairy lights dangle from the window top, looking like illuminated snowflakes falling on the village.

~~~

It worked. All of it.

Minutes after Harry flips the general store's *Closed* sign to *Open*, there's a quick knock on that door.

"We're open! Come on in," Harry calls from where he's helping his mother stack a pile of burlap placemats imprinted with Christmas wreaths.

"Good morning, Harry," a woman's voice says from the doorway.

A friendly woman's voice that he recognizes. It's Joyce, from Addison's town hall.

"Can you come outside?" she asks, her head poking through the half-opened door. Her auburn hair is windblown; her coat's faux-fur collar, upturned. "I've got things all set up out here, because, well … Congratulations, Harry! Dane's General Store won the Window Wonderland contest this year."

"Well, I'll be," Harry says, right as his mother gives a *Whoop!* In two seconds flat, she's grabbing her movie camera and heading for the door. Lifting his fleece-lined cargo jacket off a wall hook, Harry rushes outside, too.

There, in a whir of camera flashes; and handshakes from town dignitaries; and an interview from an *Addison*

116

Weekly reporter; and, yes, his own mother's movie-camera filming, Harry does it. Standing beside the *Congratulations* sign too large to fit inside the store, he accepts the significant town trophy for Winning Winter Window.

"You know what this means, Harry," Joyce from town hall says later, when the crowd thins.

If only Joyce knew what it means—everything, to him. He briefly closes his eyes to stem the sudden tears there. Tears of happiness, but sad tears, too. Tears because his pop's not standing proud beside him, his arm around Harry's shoulder. Today, Dane's General Store finally earned the town recognition that Norman had always sought.

"What it means," Joyce is saying, "is publicity! And lots of it. Dane's gets top billing on next year's town calendar. You've got the coveted cover spot."

"Excellent," Harry says.

"This is the image we'll be using." Joyce hands him a framed photograph of the general store. It was taken in recent twilight hours, when the white Christmas lights twinkled, and snow dusted the windowpanes, behind which the store's model train chugged past bottle-brush trees and through that ceramic village set in those tufts of cotton. "Your window display has the *quintessential* New England look that clinched it. The classic décor, and Americana charm. Just beautiful. Extra special this year, Harry."

Suddenly there's a tap on his shoulder, and Harry turns to see his mother slipping her movie camera into its case. "Got to run. And Joyce! Oh, it's *so* good seeing you again. But Emma needs me to watch the kids this morning."

"Okay, Ma," Harry tells her with a quick hug. "Thanks for coming in today."

"Toodle-oo!" she calls back after Joyce gives her a quick hug, too.

With his mother hurrying away down the cobblestone sidewalk, Harry helps Joyce roll up the *Congratulations* sign.

"How *is* your mom doing these days?" Joyce asks him. "I know it's been a sad year for her, because we all really miss your dad. Norm was quite a guy."

"She's doing better, Joyce. What helped is that Mom actually moved out of the barn apartment behind the store, where she lived with my father for the past few years. Emma and Garrett got an in-law suite set up in their house, and my mother lives there now."

"Oh, wonderful! I'm sure she's happy being so close to her daughter and grandchildren."

"She is."

"Changes, changes. Sometimes life throws them at us whether we like it or not," Joyce says as she hefts her tote bag up on her shoulder. "Well listen, Harry. It's been so nice working with you, *and* your father, all these years for different town events. But today? I must bid you farewell, because I have news, too."

"Everything's okay, I hope?"

"Yes. Everything's very *good*, actually. Just more of those life changes. I'll be retiring at the end of the month, so I won't be running the town competitions next year."

"Seriously?"

Joyce gives a reluctant nod. "It's a bittersweet time for me. I loved working with the local businesses, and had lots of fun over the years. But it's also time for new journeys now. Maybe see some of the world, while I still can."

"That's terrific, Joyce. You deserve it." Harry reaches over and shakes her gloved hand. "But we'll miss you, *and* your competitions … Best Scarecrow, Best Carved Pumpkin. I'll tell you, Pop lived for those contests."

"Well, I'm sure Norm's smiling down on your big win today. And don't you worry. The town is hiring a new Addison event planner next year. I'll leave all my notes behind for whoever replaces me. Hopefully, those town competitions will pick up without a hitch." Joyce clasps his hand in both of hers, giving a squeeze and telling him, *You take care.* Then she collects her bags and heads off to her car.

Harry watches her go, all while wondering about his own life. His own changes. This past year wasn't easy, saying goodbye to Pop first, then getting back to work at the store. Some days were painfully difficult, riddled with sad thoughts and doubts. *Was he right to carry on Dane's solo now? Should he have closed up the place? Made a career change? Moved?*

Then there were other days when Harry would round a corner in the store and see a fleeting shadow. Or when he'd close up at night and the wind sounded like his father's voice. Some days, lonely days, came when there was no one to turn to with his business questions.

But other days? Good days like today? Well, there have been more and more of those recently.

Standing alone on the sidewalk on this cold December morning, Harry first looks at the shining trophy set on the porch rail. Then, well, then Harry glances up at the Dane's

General Store sign mounted atop the porch overhang. He remembers a certain day fifteen years ago when he was only a college student and his father was a brand-new storekeeper. It was a December day when two tall ladders were propped against the building as he and his father raised, measured and hung that sign together. Beneath the store's name were three smaller words his father proudly pointed out—*Storekeeper: Norman Dane.*

Now, Harry's thirty-four years old. So much time has passed since then. Looking at that sign, there are new painted words beneath the store name. Three simple words that most notably signify how his own life has since changed.

Storekeeper: Harry Dane

eighteen

The Eighteenth Winter

SOMETIMES HARRY JUST KNOWS. WHEN it happens, there's no fighting it. And today's one of those times. One of those days when he'll get nothing done in the store except to assist, guide and talk to customers. Direct them to the right aisle, the right gadget. Demonstrate how to fill a bird feeder, or maneuver a jar opener, or assemble a dollhouse. No paperwork will be completed in the back office; no inventory will be ordered or stocked on the shelves. Barely a break will be taken, by him or his help.

Not on this day. The store is always mobbed on Black Friday, but on Small Business Saturday? Even more so. Especially with the advertised offer of a free *Dane's General Store* T-shirt to the first twenty-five customers making a purchase. The entrance door opens so often, the bell above it jingles and jangles like it's ringing out a Christmas tune.

So there's nothing—nothing at all—for Harry to do

today except roll up his flannel shirtsleeves and help bag stocking stuffers and holiday lights and ornament hooks and wreath hangers. Cheeses and brownies and jellied spice drops. Earmuffs and mittens and knit scarves. The smartest thing he did this year was adding another cash register. Bags of bows and rolls of wrapping paper are flying off the shelves. The stack of snow shovels is shrinking.

"Dane's General," Harry says when he manages to answer the ringing store phone near the registers.

"Harry. It's Emma."

"Emma. Really swamped here right now."

"I know. But I forgot to tell you that tenant is arriving this morning."

"Tenant?" he asks when an old friend walks in—*jingle, jangle*—and waves to him.

"For the barn apartment," Emma's explaining while Harry waves back. "I told her to get the keys from you. She's moving in today."

"Today? Do you know how crazy it is here? It's Small Business Saturday, Emma." He holds up a hand to a customer asking about holiday potholders.

"But it's the first weekend she could get a moving van. Try to show her around when she gets there? She rented Mom and Dad's old apartment only off the photographs I emailed her."

"I'll keep an eye out for her, Em. And I'll give her the keys. But we're too busy here for me to do much else. She'll have to fend for herself."

"Okay, fine. I'll be there at the store to help out later this afternoon."

"Wait, Emma," Harry says to a dial tone now. "*What's her name?*" he whispers while hanging up the phone, then getting back to business. To directing the waiting shopper to potholders and oven mitts. To chewing the fat with his friend Frank Lombardo. To manning the soda fountain for a bit before getting more snow shovels from the storage room upstairs, then pouring more hot drinks.

So all's good. From where he stands serving hot cocoa and coffee, Harry looks out at the shoppers milling about on the checkerboard floor. Customers are inspecting hand-carved birdhouses, trying on sweatshirts, sitting on swivel stools. They toss a greeting or question his way, too.

Point me to the jigsaw puzzles?
Third row over.
Have a nice Thanksgiving, Harry?
You bet, Mrs. Crenshaw. At my sister's place this year.
Get in any more of those glittery snow deer? The whittled ones?
Pete Davis is dropping off an order this afternoon. Check back.
Where are the hand mixers?
Kitchen row, back of the aisle.
Hey, Harry. I'm about to start the horse-and-carriage rides. Dane's is first stop on the morning route.
Excellent, Derek. Line's forming outside.

All the while, Harry pours and talks and bags and explains and assists and wipes the counter and starts more coffee brewing.

123

Addison's Main Street is bustling. Shoppers with packages hurry along cobblestone sidewalks. Christmas lights shine all around storefronts, and families stop at window displays of snow villages and ice-skating scenes. In the vintage wedding shop? A bride-and-groom mannequin couple spins in a slow waltz beneath twinkling lights. The groom wears a black tux and tails. The bride's long satin gown swirls behind her, and elbow-length velvet gloves reach up her arms as faux snow falls around them.

Yes, bells are ringing; fresh-cut trees are strapped to tops of cars; and on the sidewalks, people in a sea of wool caps and fluffy scarves and colorful parkas sip cocoa and call out greetings as they dash here and there.

It's so busy, she actually has to drive around The Green three times, slowly, before a parking space opens up in front of Dane's General Store. Quickly, she pulls in and turns off the car's engine.

"Made it," she says, then takes a long breath and digs a slip of paper out of her purse. But a particular rhythmic sound has her looking in the rearview mirror then. "How do you like that?" she whispers right as a horse clip-clops past while pulling a festive carriage of bundled-up folks.

Taking a minute to get her bearings, she rereads the newspaper ad that brought her here in the first place. *Apartment for Rent. In restored vintage barn filled with charm and cheer. Two bedrooms, modern kitchen, living room, spacious loft. Lots of New England character in stone fireplace, vaulted ceilings, original barnwood and beams. Available immediately. Call Emma.*

Which she did. She called Emma a few weeks ago and the lease was emailed and signed. Leaning to the left, she tries to see around to the rear of the general store, which is where this barn apartment should be. But from where she's sitting in her car, and with that horse-drawn carriage letting off riders, and with elves giving out candy canes on the store's porch, all she really sees is the general store itself. It's in an old two-story farmhouse. The dark brown wood-planked siding and white-trimmed windows give it a rustic feel. She thinks that if the apartment is as quaint as the store, it'll be perfect.

Finally, her eyes look up at the Dane's General Store sign mounted over the porch. Beneath the sign's listing of postcards, gifts, coffee and other sundries, she sees just what she's looking for. *Storekeeper: Harry Dane.*

Gathering her gloves, shoulder bag and duffel, she gets out of the car. The air is chilly, so she half zips her parka, gives another long look at the general store, then walks up the porch steps, opens the door and goes inside.

⌒◯

Whenever that bell jangles over the door, Harry manages a glance over. The stream of shoppers—families and teens and couples and singles—is constant today. Many faces are familiar, some not so much. When a young woman wearing jeans and a fur-trimmed black parka walks in, he looks, then looks again. Her blonde hair is twisted back in a low bun; her tan ankle boots match her tan turtleneck sweater. A large purse is slung over one shoulder, and a full duffel hangs over the other. No, it's not anyone he knows, so he continues helping an uncertain man pick out scented candles for his wife.

125

But he keeps an eye on the woman in the black jacket. Now she's lifting a box of old-fashioned glass ornaments. She's also got him wondering something … *Is that duffel some sort of luggage, and she's the tenant moving into the barn apartment?* Problem is, Harry's too busy to ask as he's scooping out penny candy for a mother and her two kids. The most he can manage is another glance as the woman in the parka moves on to the shelf of Christmas cards.

"Lollipops, and some bubble gum," the mother is meanwhile telling Harry. "And oh, yes," she says, pointing to a large jar, "butterscotch discs for me. And some red licorice."

So Harry scoops and bags and glimpses that other woman in the fur-trimmed black jacket purchasing a box of Christmas cards. He folds the bag of penny candy and sends the mother and her children along to the cash register as the mystery woman finishes paying there. She looks around then, before taking her cards and purse and duffel over to the soda fountain and sitting on the only empty stool.

"Can I help you with something?" Harry asks her as he walks behind the counter.

"Yes! A hot chocolate, please," she says while unzipping that parka and loosening it around her shoulders. "With *lots* of marshmallows. I'm celebrating today."

Harry reaches for a mug on the shelf before looking briefly back over his shoulder. The woman's smile is wide, her eyes sparkling. "What's the occasion?" he asks, filling her mug with steaming hot cocoa.

"That I'm finally back in town after being away for a *very* long time."

Harry adds a hefty scoop of mini marshmallows into

the frothy drink. "Is that right?" he asks, looking up from the marshmallow-laden mug.

This woman, leaning on the counter, nods. Nods, then pulls a piece of paper out of that mega shoulder bag of hers. "I'm renting an apartment in town. Right here, actually. And I'm looking for a ... Harry Dane?"

"Well, now." Harry sets her cocoa mug on the counter in front of her. "That'd be me."

"Oh, okay. Because your sister, Emma? She said I should ask for you," the woman tells him. "I'm renting your barn apartment."

"Of course. Emma mentioned you'd be here today."

The woman tips her head and extends a hand. A thin gold bangle shows beneath her coat sleeve. "Pleased to meet you, Harry. I'm Sadie," she says right as he takes her hand and gives a shake. "Sadie Welles."

⟡

Again, life proves it to Harry. Some things you never see coming. And what Harry never saw coming this time was two words.

Two words that swung the past seventeen winters right back at him, nearly knocking him off his feet. He may have even stumbled while shaking Sadie's hand over the soda fountain counter.

Two words that his mind whispered again and *again* as he put on his cargo jacket and told his new tenant she could drive her car around back, to where the apartment was. "Just follow the driveway all the way to the end, then veer left."

127

Two words that were like a spirit haunting his every minute while he showed her the garage on the side of the barn. While he unlocked the apartment door and turned to her waiting behind him. Waiting in her sleek black parka with its fur-lined hood. Waiting and watching as he dropped the keys on the ground while giving them to her—right as the moving van backed down the general store's driveway to the barn apartment.

When Harry returned to the store, those two words ran through his mind, over and over. And whenever he helped customers bring packages to their cars, Harry stole a look down the driveway to that moving van. Furniture—furniture that belonged to someone he never dreamt he'd *ever* lay eyes on—was carried piece by piece into the barn apartment with its vaulted wood-planked ceilings. The apartment with its stone fireplace reaching to that ceiling on one end, and with a windowed loft looking out onto a small woodland area on the other.

Those two words he never saw coming? They never stopped repeating and replaying in his disbelieving mind all afternoon—until his sister, Emma, took over for the evening shift.

Even then, the two words followed him home. From room to room that night after dinner, as he walked from his kitchen, to his living room, to one particular Queen Anne end table whose drawer he opens now, those two words echoed in his thoughts.

Two words that he finally—*finally*—says aloud after reaching into the end table drawer for the top card, opening it to be absolutely sure, and first *silently* reading the name penned beneath the Christmas greeting.

"Sadie," he says then, before setting the card down. Walking to his living room window and looking out onto the dark street, he stops there and shakes his head. "Sadie Welles."

nineteen

OUT OF SIGHT, OUT OF mind, Harry figures. Emma checked in with Sadie Sunday evening to be sure she was settled into the barn apartment. She was, and so that's that. As far as Harry is concerned, the apartment has a tenant. One who's quiet, and respectful, and will come and go as she pleases. He and Sadie won't have any more inadvertent bump-ins turning his conscience on end—like their meeting did over the weekend.

And with their paths not likely to cross much again, there's no reason to explain things to Sadie. To muddle his way through the story of her holiday cards mistakenly arriving at his house all these years. No reason to give some bungled explanation of why he never dropped her a line. Never set the record straight.

Yes, Harry Dane thinks he can handle it. Thinks he can handle Sadie Welles being back in Addison, Connecticut. He'll be busy with the general store, and she'll live her own life—whatever that might be. He'll simply adjust to her renting the barn apartment behind the general store and leave well enough alone.

Until her Christmas card arrives.

It takes a few days, but on Wednesday, there it is. Smack-dab in his mailbox, tucked in with bills and a department store catalog. He can't miss it. Can't miss the names on the envelope: Lorrie and Allan. So now Harry's predicament has changed. *Now*, he can do one of *two* things. Personally return the card to Sadie when he goes to the general store for the afternoon shift. He could offer a vague explanation and be done with this tricky situation.

Or, option two. He can open Sadie's card with his lunch.

Which he does.

But not at first. First he just looks at the sealed envelope in his kitchen. While putting ham and cheese on two slices of whole-grain bread, he glances at the card on the countertop. While shredding lettuce and slicing tomato, his eyes steal another look. While slathering on mayo and mustard, one more glance.

When he sits at the farm table, he does it. Digs into the sandwich with a double bite, and rips into the envelope, too. Slices it open with his knife and pulls out the card. Okay, so this cover it's a card he actually recognizes—from the box Sadie bought at Dane's General. The watercolor illustration is of a snowcapped mailbox with its red flag flipped up. But instead of an actual metal flag, a bright red cardinal perches in its place.

Before reading on, Harry convinces himself that this *is* the right thing to do. Maybe something Sadie's written will help him decide what to tell her. Finally, he looks inside the card and sees the familiar cursive beneath the holiday verse. He drags a finger across her words.

Greetings, Lorrie!

See the postmark on my envelope? I'm back in Addison! Once settled in, I'll stop by to see you. Oh, Lorrie. All snowy roads lead home at Christmastime, don't they?

All my love to you and Allan,
Sadie

Her words don't help Harry.

As a matter of fact, if things can get even worse, they just did. Harry sets down the card and cleans up his lunch things with a sense of dread. Dread because at any random time now, Sadie will show up at his door. Stand on his Craftsman bungalow's front porch. Show up with an expectant smile on her face, and hope in her heart.

He supposes it's good that he at least knows this. But if he'd done the right thing years ago, the whole situation would never have come to pass. He'd never have to fret about Sadie Welles showing up at his home.

Maybe just getting to work will help ease his mind.

It doesn't. That afternoon at the general store, Harry suffers the consequences of his new worry. And his customers let him know it.

When he rings up wrong prices: *Is that wrapping paper fourteen ninety-nine, Harry? I thought the ticket said four ninety-nine.*

When he drops coins while giving change: *Oops! Butter fingers, Harry.*

When he forgets about a customer waiting for help: *You tired today, Harry?*

When he leaves a nearly empty coffeepot on the burner and the scent of singed coffee fills the store: *Something on your mind, Harry? You seem ... distracted.*

Distracted. Yes, that's the word—to put it mildly. Distracted by a certain Christmas card.

By a certain apartment tenant.

By the jangling bell over the store's door.

By the way he turns from whatever he's doing—adding marshmallows to cocoa; stacking sacks of birdseed; sweeping light snow off the front walkway; pointing out differences between ergonomic and telescopic snow shovels—to see precisely who's walking into Dane's General Store.

To see if it's Sadie Welles.

Sadie's always thought of Addison as a snow-globe town. And with the light flurry falling now, it's like someone just gave that magical globe a shake. While driving through town Wednesday afternoon, whispers of snowflakes swirl around familiar landmarks: Whole Latte Life Coffee Café, with its frosted windowpanes; the local nursery's garden statues cloaked in those white crystals; historical Cape Cod houses and saltbox colonials rising behind the dancing flakes. Bare maple tree branches wear a glove of white snow. Yes, the whole town's as pretty as she remembers.

Especially so is the covered bridge. Her tires thunk over the planked floor until she emerges on the other side. Looking at the familiar imposing captains' houses set back on large yards, and farmhouse porches decorated with garland and wreaths, well, Sadie might as well be thumbing through a cherished scrapbook—one that has her sigh with each charming image.

This journey is one she's dreamt of ever since she was sixteen and got her driver's license: to drive these Connecticut country roads to one certain destination. Now, after all these years, she's doing it. She's going to stop by and see her old neighbors, Lorrie and Allan. It'll be so nice to visit with them again. To talk a little, to reminisce.

Slowly, Sadie turns onto Birch Lane. First she passes a small Victorian, then a shingled ranch. Her old family home, a Garrison colonial, is next. And finally, as if she'd never left the neighborhood, there's Lorrie's house: the olive-green Craftsman bungalow. It's clapboard sided, with a shingled second-story front dormer and a large stone chimney. And, oh, that front porch. How many hours did she and Lorrie while away sitting on the porch swing there? Pulling into the driveway, Sadie thinks that all they'd need is a comfy blanket to sit there now, once more.

So she parks in the driveway and hurries to the porch. Stamping off her snowy boots on the mat, she gives a quick knock and steps back to wait. And watch the door. And listen for footsteps from inside the house. In a minute, she knocks again on the wood-planked front door. Its white paint is distressed, with some of the wood grain showing through. Lorrie must've refinished the old

134

wood door that used to be here. And the whole look of the distressed white planks perfectly suits the bungalow.

When no one answers that rustic door, though, Sadie walks across the porch to the living room windows. Cupping her hands to her face, she looks inside. The room is shadowy on this cloudy December day, and it's hard to make out any details other than the big stone fireplace across the room. Looks like there's a tall Christmas tree beside it, too.

"Darn." Sadie checks her watch then. "But no one's home." Leaving the front porch, she slowly heads toward her car. Glancing over her shoulder to that beautiful porch, it's obvious that Lorrie hasn't finished her Christmas decorating yet—which is a little unlike her. No lights are strung outside; no candles stand in the windows. So when Sadie comes back again, she knows just what to bring: a large balsam wreath, perfect for that antiqued front door.

∽◯

It happens all the time. A little snow falls and the general store gets busy. Folks hurry in looking for shovels for walkways, or ice scrapers for their cars. Shoppers buy mittens. They talk up the weather. Late Wednesday afternoon, Harry listens while stacking boxes of ornaments in the decorating row.

Heard it from the man himself, one customer says.

The man? another asks.

Leo Sterling, chief meteorologist. Said to get out our shovels, and put away the rakes!

135

I guess that's what we'll be needing, from the looks of those snowflakes.

So Harry rushes to the stockroom and brings out an armful of new snow shovels. He neatly stands them in metal shovel holders on a wall rack. By the time he's done, that bell's jangled over the door several times as customers keep breezing into the store.

Unfortunately, this time one of those customers is a familiar woman—one he's actually nervous about seeing. Her blonde hair is down today, falling over the back of her black parka as she sits on a swivel stool at the soda fountain. She's apparently bought the *Addison Weekly* and is perusing the newspaper's headlines. When she looks up just then, and looks directly at him while giving a small wave, Harry walks over.

"How are you today … Sadie?" he asks, as if he's uncertain. As if he doesn't know eighteen years of personal facts about this woman. "It's Sadie, right?"

Sadie nods. "I'm good, Harry. Can I have a coffee, with cream? To go. Thought I'd bring it back to the apartment and catch up on the local news there." She briefly holds up the newspaper.

Harry lifts the decanter and fills a paper mug. "Everything working out okay since you moved in?"

"Hm? Oh, yes," Sadie says while looking up from an article that's got her attention. "Your barn apartment's so lovely. And I saw a deer in the wooded area outside the back windows!"

"That's nice. I'm glad you're settled." Harry puts the steaming mug in front of her as she's drawn back to whatever town story she's reading. "Nothing else today?"

he asks while jotting out her check. The sooner he moves on, the sooner his conscience will quiet down. "We're good?"

"Not really," Sadie vaguely says, her eyes still skimming some front-page article.

"Something's wrong then? But I thought—"

"Oh, no. *We're* good. But I'm really bothered by this article. Did you see it?" She turns the paper around and shows him the headline: *Hark! Christmas on Addison's Green Will Be Dark.*

"It's true." Harry glances at the paper's front page. "Addison usually makes a big to-do with their tree-lighting ceremony. But we've got no town tree this year."

Sadie sips her coffee, then loosens her parka around her shoulders. "Well, that's very sad. A New England town green with no Christmas tree? No twinkling lights?"

"We *had* a tree," Harry explains. "A big one, soaring to the sky. That tree was a beauty, all right. But this past August? Lightning struck it. Split the old pine in half."

Sadie quickly spins her stool around, as if she'll catch a glimpse of that split tree out on The Green. Harry glances out, too. Colonial-style lampposts surround the wishing fountain area. But there's a large, vacant spot where the tree once stood. As he pours two cups of cocoa for an older couple, he tells Sadie, "They're hoping to plant a new tree in the spring."

Sadie looks over her shoulder at him, then looks out the window once more. When she finally spins back on her stool, she's still obviously bothered. "But a *dark* Christmas? It says here," she goes on, looking down at the article, "that without a festive gathering place, it'll be a lonesome Christmas for the town of Addison."

Harry shrugs. "I suppose. At least it'll be lonesome on The Green, without that big tree drawing carolers, and sightseers, and picture-takers," he says before setting down the two hot cocoas for his waiting customers.

"And you know something? I just may be able to fix that." Sadie pulls her cell phone from her shoulder bag. "I'm going to call the town manager."

Harry's not too sure what the town manager can do for her. Just then, a cashier calls him over for a price check. So he waves to Sadie, who waves back mid-dialing. But he walks away slowly, so that between the jangling bell over the door; and a friend calling out, *Hey, Harry*; and the customer at the register saying the window candles don't have a price on them, he hears snatches of Sadie's conversation. Actually, it's similar to the snatches of her life he's read about in her cards over the years. Just bits and pieces. Just enough.

Warren Clark? It's Sadie. Sadie Welles ... Town Christmas tree is gone ... Unacceptable ... A tree's the shining crown ... At Christmastime, people need light to believe ... Listen ... I have an idea.

twenty

THE NEXT DAY IS ONE of those rare times when everything's going right. Sadie's boss loved her proposed idea for a new holiday event in Addison. Now Sadie can spread the word about it at the town's Small Business Christmas Party this weekend.

And her apartment? It couldn't be cozier. With its sliding barn door leading to a deck out back; and the crackling fires she lights in the stone fireplace; and the rough-hewn ceiling beams; and the patch of woods outside her bedroom window. Sometimes she even hears the hoot of a barred owl, soft and melodic in the night.

Not to mention the festive vibes of this quaint New England town. She'd forgotten how the folks here truly take the holiday to heart. More and more looped garland and strings of lights and living room twinkling Christmas trees show up with each passing day.

What it all does this Thursday evening, all of this

goodness, is this: It has her stop at Cooper Hardware Store. Whenever she's passed their old-fashioned tree lot with light bulbs strung crisscrossed above it, she's been tempted to pull in. Now she has a reason to.

"Can I help you?" a man asks as he approaches.

"Yes, actually." Sadie looks up from where she'd leaned close to a tree just to inhale that sweet pine-tree scent. She turns to the man, who's dressed in jeans, a cargo jacket and backward baseball cap. "Do you have any wreaths?"

"You bet. Come on," he says, motioning his gloved hand. "I'll show you."

It's cold, with a wintry wind picking up. Sadie wraps her knit scarf around her neck and follows this man past a few rows of trees before veering to the side of the lot. There, looking like a watercolor painting straight off a Christmas card, is the wreath display. Balsam wreaths of all sizes hang from mounted latticework. Some of the wreaths have looped bows; some shiny ornaments; some frosted apples; others white-tipped pinecones. In the wind, soft boughs of the wreaths rustle; long ribbons flutter.

"You have a look around," the man tells her.

"There are so many, and they're all beautiful!" She stops in front of a wreath dotted with red berries. "It'll be hard to choose."

"Just be sure to pick the one that speaks to you."

It doesn't take long. A certain wreath speaks to Sadie right away. Its simplicity suits the Craftsman bungalow's distressed-white door. The wreath she lifts off the rack is country chic, with pinecones nestled along the bottom.

And tucked in the middle is a little white tin house, with several window cut-outs.

But what clinches it for Sadie is that the top window is in the shape of a heart. Because it feels like her own heart—that little cut-out does—filled with hope and love.

After she pays and sets the wreath in her car's trunk, she drives across town toward Birch Lane again. Now she's actually glad that Lorrie and Allan weren't home yesterday, because she was empty-handed when she stopped by.

This is better. This time, after all these years away, Sadie has a gift for Lorrie's home. The perfect country-style wreath to hang on that rustic front door.

So yesterday's disappointment has turned into holiday excitement as Sadie drives through Olde Addison in the evening light. Imposing homes line the street: slate-blue and brick-red colonials with paned windows and arched doorways. There are garland-wrapped lampposts, and tiny white lights draped along picket fences. The whole way there, passing every historical Federal and timeworn Dutch colonial, Sadie can't wait to see her old friends— this time bringing a beautiful gift for their home.

"*Everything happens for a reason,*" Sadie whispers as she turns onto Birch Lane.

❧

The moment when Sadie knocks at his door is imminent. Harry wishes it would just happen already—once and for all. Then he'd be done with this endless waiting. With his charade. With telling Sadie his sad truth.

Instead, after receiving her Christmas card to Lorrie and Allan, he's done nothing but tidy up. He wipes crumbs from the counter, wraps the toaster cord, sweeps the kitchen floor. That done, he returns to Sadie's card. There's no denying that she'll show up at his house; it's just a matter of when. Maybe there's some clue in her words. Some indication of exactly which day her visit might happen.

Greetings, Lorrie!

See the postmark on my envelope? I'm back in Addison! Once settled in, I'll stop by to see you. Oh, Lorrie. All snowy roads lead home at Christmastime, don't they?

All my love to you and Allan,
Sadie

Nothing. She's as vague as can be. So now the waiting's driving Harry crazy. It has him dust the tambour clock on the fireplace mantel next, then look out the living room windows. She could show up tonight, or next week. He walks to the curb to get his mail, and sneaks a look down the street for headlights coming toward his house. Hanging up his jacket back inside, he then looks out the window once more. Puts two pillar candles on silver pedestals in the dining room, and glances out the paned windows there as he does.

All the while, he wonders. Should he have at least told Sadie that her *latest* Christmas card arrived at his house? Should he have mentioned something, *anything*, when she sat at the soda fountain yesterday? Said some words to break the ice. To let her down easy.

But what could he say, right there in the general store? *Listen, Sadie. For eighteen winters, I've been reading your personal Christmas cards. I meant to drop you a line ... Planned to send ...*

Doesn't matter now. Not when the doorbell chimes at that very moment. Quickly, he puts the broom in the closet. Stops in front of a mirror and draws a hand down his unshaven jaw. Gives a once-over to his black cardigan over a white tee and black jeans. Takes a breath and turns up his sweater cuffs.

Finally, with eighteen years of regret barreling straight at him, Harry walks down the hallway, puts his hand on the doorknob and stops. Just freezes right there, because this is it. This is the moment eighteen winters led to. He hesitates and figures he can either ignore the person on the other side of the door, or wing it. Just get through whatever conversation will happen—if he opens that door.

Without any more thinking, he turns the knob and does it.

⌒✑○

Harry first sees Sadie's face. He sees the way her expression drops, too, when she looks at *him*—instead of this Lorrie woman. Gone is Sadie's brief, hopeful anticipation.

"Harry?" she asks.

Harry tips his head. "Sadie?" he asks back. Now, now he sees the rest. Sees her long blonde hair falling over the shoulders of a camel wool coat. Sees the straight gray pants and gray sweater beneath that coat. Sees her arm looped through a large balsam wreath. Finally, his gaze returns to her uncertain eyes. There's no escaping those.

"Why, I thought ..." Sadie steps back and takes a long look at the bungalow's doorway and house number. Then she looks back over her shoulder, in the direction of the Garrison colonial next door. "You live ... *here?*"

"I do." He opens the door further. "What are you doing here?" he asks, as if he doesn't know. As if he hasn't been walking on pins and needles since reading her latest card. As if he doesn't know pretty much every milestone of her entire life. "I mean, I'm surprised to see you, that's all."

"Well, I came to visit an old neighbor. You see, someone I know used to ..." she says, vaguely looking toward the next-door colonial again, then giving a quick shake of her head. "Maybe I'm mistaken."

That wreath she's holding is weighing down her arm. So Harry steps outside onto the porch. "Can I take that for you?"

"Oh, this. Thanks," she says as he lifts the balsam wreath. "It was for my old neighbor. Lorrie. Do you know ..." She squints up at him in the illumination of the porch light. "This is *really* your house?"

He nods.

"I don't mean to be nosy, but ... have you lived here a long time?"

"I bought the place a few years back." Harry shifts the wreath to his other arm. "Would you like to come in? Sit down and, I don't know ..."

"What? No, no. That's okay." She looks over at the porch swing, then at Harry again. "The people you

144

bought the house from … was it someone named Lorrie? And Allan?"

"No." He *could* tell her the truth of it all, right now. Could just come clean about opening her holiday cards. But Sadie looks too upset. So now doesn't seem like the right time. "I actually bought the house from my parents, when they downsized."

"Oh. But did you ever get Christmas cards … Well, I mean. Oh, look at me blabbering. I'm just really thrown. Because I thought a dear friend of mine lived here. Or *used* to, anyway. A long time ago." A sad smile passes over Sadie's face before she suddenly turns and hurries down the porch steps.

"Sadie! Wait," Harry calls after her.

"I'm truly sorry to bother you, Harry."

When she turns back to him, she swipes a strand of hair—or maybe a tear—off her cheek. In the evening light, it's hard to tell. She stands on Harry's front walkway. Beyond her, candles flicker in the Tudor's windows across the street.

"Are you sure you don't want to come in?" Harry asks. "Have a coffee? Warm up, maybe?"

Sadie looks at the colonial next door, then at Harry standing on his porch. "No." She takes a quick breath. "Again, I'm so sorry—and *really* embarrassed to show up like this. At your door, I mean."

"It's no problem." Harry walks to the top porch step and watches her. What he sees now—her distress—is all his fault. It's the result of his eighteen-year mistake. Of his silence. Of his taking Sadie Welles' Christmas cards for granted. He's got to fix this, now. Good timing or not, it's the right thing to do. "Sadie, listen. There's something you should, well … I can ex—"

"I really have to go." Sadie turns and briskly walks toward her car. "Goodnight, Harry," she calls back over her shoulder.

"But I have to tell—" And he sees it, how she squints at his house and hesitates for a moment before picking up her pace. And he sees the large, heavy wreath hooked over *his* arm now. "Sadie!" he calls out. "Wait! Your wreath."

Standing at her car's open door, she looks over at him, pauses, then gives a slight wave. "That's okay. You keep it."

Before Harry can object, or give the wreath back, or insist they talk so that he can *finally* explain himself, Sadie Welles gets in her car and is gone. Dashes off like a sudden snow squall sweeping in with gusty winds, and sweeping out just as suddenly.

Here one minute, gone the next.

twenty-one

A FEW NIGHTS LATER, HARRY doesn't notice her at first. Not with all the festivities going on at the Addison Boathouse. If he thought the two-story building looked grand outside with its white lights and wreaths on every door, he was wrong. Inside the ballroom, Frank Lombardo went all out for the town-sponsored Small Business Christmas Party. A tall Christmas tree towers in the middle of the dance floor. The tree's boughs are tipped with flocked white snow; pinecones and clusters of cream baby's breath nestle in the branches; white lights twinkle. Swags of green garland loop around the window frames and across the vaulted, beamed ceiling. More tiny lights dangle from the exposed ductwork pipes overhead. Fine linens and sparkling china cover the dinner tables scattered around the room.

And the people? They're dressed to the nines—women in dresses soft as velvet, or glimmering with sequins; men in suits, and vests, wearing holiday-red boutonnieres.

Yes, the boathouse is hopping this Saturday night, with music, laughter and conversation, and good food, too.

So it takes a while before Harry notices her. Notices Sadie Welles. But he doesn't approach her. It would be difficult to, anyway, with the way she's flitting from one table to another. He keeps an eye on her, though. As he walks over to the Cooper Hardware table to talk with Derek, he notices Sadie shaking hands with Vera Sterling at the Snowflakes and Coffee Cakes table. When Harry turns just so, he hears bits of Sadie's talk with Vera.

Businesses sponsor the event. Mostly by donating lanterns.

And when Harry walks over to George Carbone at The Main Course's table, he hitches his head in a slight nod when Sadie catches his eye. He also hears more of her voice pleading her case about … something.

In return, you'd be promoted with event publicity. Newspaper ads, posters.

So something's going on. Something big, as far as Harry can tell. People are captivated by whatever Sadie's explaining. When Harry stops to say hello to Dave at the Dave's Auto Body table, Sadie's moved to Amy Trewist's Wedding Wishes table. Sadie's leaning in close and speaking very seriously—all while Amy listens and nods. Sadie also gives Harry a small smile when she notices him watching once more. But just for a second. Just until she's then typing something into her cell phone at Amy's prompting.

As a matter of fact, every time Harry spots Sadie, it's

the same thing. She speaks intently, explains something, then takes down information and is all smiles as she moves on. From one table, to another, then another. Suitcase Escapes shares a table with Vagabond Vintage, where Sadie chats with the boutique's owner, Lindsey Haynes. Next, Felucca's Fine Gifts, then another slight nod to Harry as Sadie moves on to Sara Beth Riley at the Circa 1765 Antique Shop table. Everyone is in on some plan being talked up.

On his way to the buffet area, Harry waves to Frank Lombardo. Standing with his arms crossed over his chest, Frank's practically in shadow at the side wall, keeping an eye on the event he's managing.

"Frank," Harry says when he swings over. "Kudos, man, to you and your sister. You know how to throw a party."

Frank shakes Harry's hand. "Good to see you, guy. Yeah, the town likes everything top-shelf for its small businesses. They're Addison's lifeblood, so no expense is spared for this shindig."

There's no denying that. Even the buffet table is overloaded with choice cuts of meat, specialty vegetable platters, the works. Harry fills a plate and returns to the Dane's General Store table, where his sister sits with her husband, Garrett.

But not for long. No sooner does Harry sit down with his meal than the DJ gets everyone on their feet. "One, two, three, go!" he announces as the Electric Slide begins. The music's enough to empty most of the tables in the grand ballroom. Lining the dance floor, folks dressed in their holiday finery begin sliding and stomping. When the

DJ instructs the crowd to, "Right, tap, clap," everyone gets in the groove.

Everyone except Harry. Instead, he watches while digging into his meal. Scooping a forkful of some delicious mashed-potato concoction, he tastes a mouthful as he glances around the room.

Doesn't glance far, though. Not when he sees someone else sitting in shadow, alone. If Harry's not mistaken, she's at the Town of Addison table, where the dignitaries sponsoring the event were seated before. But now? Now they're all *bringing it down, bringing it down* on the dance floor.

Well, almost all. All except for one. Except for Sadie Welles. Sadie and a heaping plate of food, too. Sadie Welles, wearing a long-sleeved, black turtleneck sweater dress with slouchy black suede boots. Her blonde hair is in a low twist, and her eyes? Oh, those eyes are suddenly looking directly at him.

Harry, well, he clears his throat and gives a wave. When Sadie waves back from her seat, he hesitates. Standing then, he lifts his plate and his drink. Weaving through a few scootin' high-heeled dancers, he manages to safely get his food to Sadie's table.

"Like some company?" he asks.

"Sure, Harry. It's good to see you."

He nods to her then. "Is someone with you? A date, or—"

"No." She stops him right there. "It's just me."

Again, Harry hesitates as he looks at an empty seat to the left, then the right, until Sadie pulls out the chair beside hers.

"Easier to talk right here," she says. "With the music,

and all that dancing going on."

They do talk, but not much. Not at first, anyway. There's an awkwardness left over between them from the other night, when Sadie showed up at his front door. To Harry, it kind of feels like something's gone unsaid. And it has. But Sadie would have no clue about it—about his opening eighteen years' worth of her Christmas cards. And this table in shadows, in the Addison Boathouse ballroom at the Small Business Christmas Party, is not the place to broach that subject. Instead, simple niceties suffice. *How've you been?* And, *What a soiree, no?* And, *I see snow's in the forecast.*

Until finally, Harry gets to it. After a few bites of his chicken marsala and mashed potatoes dragged through mushroom sauce, and after a polite toast with Sadie, he asks what's been on his mind. "Did you ever find the address of who you were looking for? Lorrie, was it?"

"Yes! Lorrie and Allan." Sadie sips her wine, then adds, "I'm going to visit them tomorrow, actually. Believe it or not, I looked them up and they live right here in town!"

"They do? No kidding."

Sadie nods.

"Well, you were upset the other night … So I'm glad it all worked out."

"It did."

Then, silence. Oh, there's rocking music, and happy foot-stomping, but between Sadie and himself? Silence. Until Sadie breaks it this time.

"Harry," she begins. "I don't think I ever made it to your table here earlier. But, as the town's new event planner—"

"Wait," Harry says, then sets down his fork. "Event planner? You mean, you were hired to replace Joyce?"

"I was!"

"Dane's General Store partnered with Joyce for lots of town happenings," Harry says. "She held that job for many years, and is a good family friend."

"Oh, I'm glad to know that," Sadie tells him.

But more than her words, Harry notices something else. He notices how Sadie scoots her chair closer to his. Notices, too, how she briefly clasps his arm when she leans in to talk. He listens to her explain the first major event she's spearheading for the town of Addison. Her voice is soft; her words, excited.

"The event is called Light the Night," Sadie goes on. "I got the idea at your store, when you told me about the town tree being hit by lightning."

With all the sliding and clapping keeping time with the loud music, Harry hears only pieces of Sadie's plan.

> *Businesses donate lanterns.*
> *Will fill The Green with them on Christmas Eve day.*
> *Carolers, sleigh rides.*
> *For each charitable donation for a new town tree, a lantern will be lit.*
> *Won't stop until all lanterns are illuminated that night, in place of missing tree.*

"Because what's Christmas Eve, Harry, without that hopeful light shining in our lives?"

When Sadie asks that one question, Harry looks into her brown eyes, and wants to tuck back a loose strand of her silky hair. He doesn't, though. Instead, he drags a few vegetables across his plate. "It's a nice thought, Sadie. And an amazing plan."

"Really appreciate that. So I can count on you for lanterns?"

By now, he and Sadie have scooted their chairs so much that their arms press together as they sit at the table. He lifts his fork and eats a mouthful of those gravy-drenched veggies. "Dane's General will definitely donate."

"Wonderful! I'll add you to my list," she says while typing into her cell phone. "How many lanterns can you commit to?"

Harry looks long at her, at her hand hovering over the phone. At her black sweater dress. At the glimmer of a gold bangle on her wrist. At her face when she tips it toward his, waiting for his answer. "Whatever you need," he says.

As he says it, though, the DJ makes an announcement to the foot-stompin' holiday dancers. "It's time to slide into each other's arms," his voice booms across the room. "For this snowy serenade," he continues while sweeping violins bring the couples close.

"How many, did you say?" Sadie's voice is practically a whisper; her eyes glance from the romantic dancing to Harry. "I didn't hear you, over the announcement."

He picks up his wine and takes a long sip. "However many you need."

Sadie doesn't press her cell phone keypad. As a matter of fact, she sets the phone aside.

"Something wrong?" Harry asks.

"Yes. I mean, no. But, yes. You see, every business

here loves my Light the Night idea, and the donation commitments have been incredible." Again, she pauses as a couple waltzes past their table. "Problem is," Sadie explains while leaning close, "there's no designated lantern drop-off spot, before the big day. I need one place to gather them together."

"I think I can help. Let the businesses know they can leave their lanterns behind Dane's General. There's a rear delivery entrance. They can stack them there. And I'll fill up the store's cargo van, too. So they can be brought to The Green Christmas Eve day."

"That would be perfect, Harry. But I don't want to inconvenience you. Are you sure?"

It's the least he can do, he thinks. And he's finding he wouldn't mind seeing more of Sadie Welles, too. But before he says anything, a familiar voice interrupts them.

"Yoo-hoo," a woman calls out as she and her dance partner twirl past.

"My sister," Harry says, bending close to Sadie's ear. "You met her when you moved in. Emma?"

"Oh, yes!" Sadie gives a finger-wave to Emma— dancing by in the arms of a man holding her close.

"She's with her husband, Garrett. They live in town. My mother lives with them, too, actually. Watches their kids when Emma helps out at the store."

"They're close, then. Your mom and sister."

"Definitely," Harry agrees.

"And how about you?" Sadie asks.

"What about me?"

"Do you have a family? Is your wife here?"

"Not married," Harry says. "I recently took over

154

running the general store. Haven't had much time for anything else. You know, dating and all that …" After Sadie's polite smile, there's that quiet again. So Harry fills it. "Anyway, I'll let Emma know about the lantern drop-off. But she won't have any problem with it."

"Okay. I'll let my boss know, too."

"Wait. The town manager?"

"Yes, Warren," Sadie says. "Warren Clark. I'm working with him. *And* with Joyce. She came back to the office temporarily to show me the ropes and explain the events she's run. I guess there's an Apple Festival. Window Wonderland. And something called Coveside Cornucopia?"

Harry just nods, then glances at the couples slow-dancing beneath twinkling lights in the dimly lit room. "Sadie," he begins, looking at her again. "It's Christmastime." Again, he hesitates, then asks, "Dance with me?"

"Why, Harry Dane. I'd love to."

Harry stands, holds her hand and walks her to the dance floor. There, beside the grand Christmas tree, he takes her in his arms. But there's a tentativeness to their dance. Harry keeps a little distance between them as they sway and turn to the Christmas song—one about snowy windowpanes, and gleaming candles, and quietly falling in love. The whole room seems swept up in the romance of the music.

Until the song changes, and slows even further. As it does, the DJ makes an announcement that gets the crowd's full attention. "It's that time of the night," he says, his voice dropping, "to find a pretty miss you might like to kiss."

Harry knows, then. Oh, does he know. The whole

crowd knows that the kiss cam has been turned on and is scanning the dance floor. Murmurs rise. Dancers watch the large screen mounted on the far wall. Someone will be captured on that kiss cam. The moment's imminent, and everyone waits for it now.

Even Harry.

Sadie does, too; he can tell. She inches back a little, and gives him a hesitant smile. But what can he do? Nothing more than dance. Uneasily, with an eye on that darn screen as the kiss cam pans the crowd. Some people cheer when it passes over them, but that camera will only stop on one couple. So the song continues, the dancing slows.

Until it happens.

Didn't Harry just know it would happen this way, too. First he notices Sadie on the wall-mounted screen. Well, notices her long blonde hair against her black dress. It gets his attention as the camera pans the dancing couples. Problem is, the camera comes in closer, and closer.

And he knows. That darn lens has the two of them in its kissing-sights. There's no way out of this. If he hesitates, or if Sadie bows out, the boos will rise. Which might even embarrass Sadie.

So … Harry does it. He stops dancing, looks at Sadie and raises one hand to the side of her face. When she raises her own hand and rests it on top of his, he's uncertain. But as he leans closer, and whispers, *For the camera*, her smile assures him it's okay. So he raises his other hand, too, and cradles her face. Loose wisps of her hair fall over his fingers, and he kisses her. Softly, to random applause rising from the dancers.

Which gets Sadie to smile again. Harry feels that sweet

smile beneath his lips. What surprises him, though, is that right when he thought he'd pull away, their kiss deepens. Just enough to elicit a few sharp whistles in the dark room illuminated mostly by twinkling lights and shimmering candles on the tables. His and Sadie's unexpectedly intimate moment lasts another few seconds before Harry pulls away—sneaking in one more light kiss before the camera fades off and the dancing continues.

"Sadie," he says into her ear. "I hope you don't … It's just that—"

"It was nice, Harry," she whispers back.

He looks at her when she says nothing more. Looks at her for a second before holding her closer again, all while giving a slow turn as their dance goes on.

❧

Sadie sits by the window later that night. She wears her fluffy robe and cups a mug of steaming tea. Outside, the moon rises high in the cold December sky. Its glow falls on the wooded area out behind the barn apartment. Trees are snow-dusted. A babbling brook glimmers silver in the moonlight falling on it.

The view is so peaceful, she finds herself sitting here like this often. There's a certain comfort to seeing the world at rest. To seeing a deer grazing. Or snow lightly falling. To hearing the gentle *hoot-hoot* of a lone owl in the woods. All while she's in the safe warmth of her new home here. Yes, it's a comfort she's often sought in her life.

Sipping her tea, she realizes it then. Yes, it's the same

comfort she surprisingly found in Harry's arms tonight. The dancing, the startling kiss. All of it, she thinks now, all of it felt … right.

⌒∾○

"Where is it?" Harry asks. Sitting in the attic later that night, he holds a small string of lights. With his other hand, he's rummaging through a storage tote filled with a tangled mess of Christmas decorations. He's so set on getting this done, he hasn't even changed out of the dress pants, suit vest and cuffed button-down he wore dancing with Sadie. "Where did it go?" he asks again now, squinting into the tote.

Moments later, he spots it. Moving aside pinecones and a stuffed snowman and strings of gold beads, he finally finds exactly what he's looking for—a tiny battery-operated candle.

"Perfect," he says before standing and going downstairs. After putting on a jacket and wool cap, he switches on the porch light, opens the front door and steps outside. The street is quiet; the night, still. From where he stands near the porch railing, faraway stars twinkle in the dark sky.

Harry turns, then, to Sadie's big balsam wreath hanging on his wood-planked front door. The wreath's green needles are soft against the door's distressed white paint. Lifting his string of Christmas lights, he weaves them through the delicate pine boughs. With an adjustment here, a little fussing there, finally those lights look just right.

The whole time, he's painfully aware that Sadie intended this wreath for someone else. That his own

158

pathetic secret led to her sadly leaving the wreath behind. So he figures he'll make it up to her by turning this into the most beautiful wreath on the street. It's one small way of trying to fix things. Or, of trying to fix his past mistake.

He steps back and eyes the wreath before pulling the battery-operated tea-light candle from his pocket. Carefully, he props it inside the small tin house nestled in the wreath's boughs. When he flicks on the candle switch, every cut-out window in that white tin house illuminates, glowing warmly against the balsam wreath on this dark December night.

twenty-two

THE DAY'S FINALLY ARRIVED. AT last, Sadie will see her old friend—the same friend to whom she's sent a Christmas card every year for the past twenty years.

Early Sunday afternoon, Sadie puts on her fur-trimmed black parka and drives to Lorrie's house near Addison Cove. Other than their brief phone call a few days ago, they haven't spoken in two decades—though it doesn't feel it. Somehow, sending those greetings in her annual holiday cards was Sadie's way of talking. Of keeping in touch with the woman who looked after her many afternoons when she was just a girl.

The problem is, Lorrie apparently never received her annual cards. So will she mind this reunion? Does Sadie's old neighbor truly want to reconnect with the past? Now, Sadie's uncertain. Following Lorrie's directions, she takes the last left before the cove's entrance and drives down a short, narrow road. The homes here are small, but quaint. Old, but lovingly well-tended. Farmhouses and cottage bungalows with porch balustrades and gingerbread trim. Homes perfectly suited to where Sadie would imagine Lorrie and Allan might live. Still, the closer Sadie gets to the house—the last one on the street—the slower she goes. There's no denying that twenty years stand between them … between the last time Sadie and Lorrie have seen each other.

But all it takes is a smile. One smile to erase twenty years of time. Twenty years of wondering. And two days' worth of doubt.

The smile comes as soon as she turns her car into Lorrie's driveway. Her old friend is sitting on the front porch of her painted-brick ranch house. And when Sadie pulls in, Lorrie stands. She looks to be in her late sixties now. Her shoulder-length hair is silvery and sideswept. She has on a brown fitted jacket over black trousers, with a thick scarf around her neck. She's tall, and wears small, frameless glasses.

And that smile.

It's the same warm smile Sadie remembers from all those years ago when she'd get off the school bus. Back then, Lorrie waited on her front porch to babysit her until Sadie's mother got home from work.

And just like then, Sadie smiles right back now. Smiles and hurries to this *new* porch, opening her arms and calling out, "Lorrie!"

"Sadie! Oh, sweet Sadie," Lorrie is saying as she hugs her.

Of course, the hug is so genuine, Lorrie's words so gentle, Sadie feels one thing and one thing only: like she's home again.

In a moment, Lorrie steps back and holds Sadie at arm's

161

length. "The last time I saw you, you were just a girl!"

"It's been twenty years," Sadie says with a teary nod. "I was twelve years old."

"And look at you today. All grown up, and so beautiful."

"Oh! And who's this here?" Sadie asks, bending to pet a cute little dog at their feet. Her fingers stroke the dog's soft fur.

"That's Buster. He's my rescue dog. A Sheltie mix, and he never leaves my side."

Sadie crouches down and scratches the friendly dog's fluffy ears. "Aren't you so handsome!" When Sadie looks up, she tells her old friend, "I've really missed you, Lorrie. You and Allan. You're both well?"

Lorrie nods and takes Sadie's hand. "Allan's actually at work. He's a security guard at the hospital now."

"Oh, I'm sorry I missed him."

"I'll tell him that," Lorrie assures her. "But you come sit down. Over here!" She motions to a country bench, where two cups of steaming cocoa wait on a table there. "Remember the afternoons we used to spend on my front porch? When you'd tell me about your day at school?"

Sadie can only manage another nod as Lorrie looks back at her.

"Well," Lorrie is saying as they cross the porch, "I thought we should catch up right here, first." She rubs her mittened hands together. "Then we'll go inside and sit by the fire to warm up."

"Just like the old days," Sadie says when she sits on the bench. "Oh, Lorrie, I'm so glad to have found you again."

Time passes quickly with Lorrie. They sip hot cocoa on the porch, and Sadie shares some of the life moments she'd jotted in twenty years of Christmas cards. Going away to college. Studying abroad. The jobs she's had since graduation. Buying her condo in Keene, New Hampshire. Her new job as Addison's event planner.

"So you're here in town permanently?" Lorrie asks.

"I am. I often thought about moving back here, and when this job opening came up? Well, I sold my condo and for now, live in a rustic barn apartment behind Dane's General Store. And it feels so good to be here again. I'll be helming all of Addison's townwide community events."

"That's wonderful! But no husband with you on this return trip, Sadie?" Lorrie asks over her shoulder once they move inside to talk more.

"No. I never married." Sadie follows Lorrie and Buster through the front door. In the living room, logs burn in the fireplace. A tray of cookies sits on a low table. With the antique lamps, framed paintings and worn Oriental rug, the room is pure Lorrie—historical, through and through.

"Are you seeing someone, though?" Lorrie asks when she sits in a chair and wraps a knitted throw around her shoulders. The dog curls up on the floor beside her.

"Not right now." Sadie settles on a comfortable sofa lined with fringed pillows. "Oh, there were a few fellows, Lorrie, over the years. Someone at the office," she says while pulling off her gloves. "A neighbor. But things didn't work out. I'd mentioned them in my cards to you, but …"

"How I would've loved to have received them."

"I wish you did, Lorrie. I mailed them all to your old address on Birch Lane."

"What do you suppose happened?" Lorrie asks. "The cards weren't forwarded to me. And they weren't returned to you, either?"

"No. It's very sad that they're simply lost. Or thrown away." Sadie slips out of her jacket and sets it on the couch. "They were little pieces of my life, written in notes to you."

"Well! You'll just have to fill me in on the rest. Like your mother," Lorrie says. "How is—" When Sadie simply shakes her head, Lorrie stops talking. "Oh, no," she whispers then.

"Mom died when I was in college," Sadie quietly tells her. "It was such a sad time, Lorrie. I'd mentioned it in my Christmas card that year."

"Oh, Sadie." Lorrie reaches over and squeezes Sadie's hand. "I'm so sorry I didn't receive *that* card, especially."

"Me, too. But Mom's why I also *kept* sending you the Christmas cards. It was something she and I did together, ever since I was a girl. Writing holiday cards to friends and family. Those are some of my favorite memories. Picking out beautiful cards. And buying a special pen for them. We'd sit at the kitchen table a few evenings each December and write our greetings, with Christmas music playing, maybe a candle burning. Then she'd bundle the cards with twine and off we'd go to the post office, sending our holiday love—that's how she put it. So I kept that tradition going. For her. It helped me, too, over time."

"But even when you didn't hear back from me, you kept sending cards? You never gave up?"

"No, Lorrie. I was on the move so much, living at one

address, then another, that I never *expected* a response. And Mom always said it wasn't about that. It was more about remembering special people in our hearts with little cards." Thinking of her mother fondly like this, Sadie gives Lorrie a warm smile. "She said *that's* what the holiday was all about."

"You must miss her."

"I do. Especially this time of year." Sadie gets up and walks to the Christmas tree. Even that is vintage, with its big colorful lights tucked into boughs draped with silver tinsel. She touches a glass ornament, then turns to Lorrie. "You never received *any* of my cards, though? I mean, I remember way back I sent you a copy of my high school yearbook photo?"

"I think I received some early cards, before Allan and I moved out of town. When his parents got older, we moved in with them in Eastfield. Living in another town, and at *their* address, well I'm sure some mail got lost in the shuffle."

"But what about your job?" Sadie asks when she sits again and reaches for a frosted sugar cookie from the tray. "You always loved teaching history to your students here."

"Which I continued to do. Eastfield wasn't that long of a commute. And things worked out well, because I had time off as a teacher. Summers, and winter breaks. So I helped Allan's parents around the house then. Did the gardening. And a lot of cooking. Those were busy years, for sure." Lorrie looks toward the window, then back at Sadie. "They were good people. And maybe since I never had children of my own, I enjoyed taking care of others.

You," Lorrie says with an easy nod. "Allan's folks. And now, even Buster." She reaches down and gives the dog a gentle pat.

"So what brought you back here, Lorrie?"

"Sadly, after Allan's folks passed …"

"Oh, I'm so sorry to hear this," Sadie offers.

"Thank you, dear. Anyway, Addison always felt like home, so we moved back a couple of years ago. I've retired from teaching, but I stay busy. I work part-time for the town, giving tours of the historical homes."

Which is all Sadie needs to hear. And she's not surprised, sitting in Lorrie's living room where antique mahogany nesting tables and a cherry tea cart glow beneath the afternoon sunlight. Right away, as they snack on Christmas cookies beside the fireplace, she tells Lorrie her idea for an event next year. Something about a walking excursion through Addison's historical houses all decorated for the holidays. There could be detailed maps of neighborhoods, and pamphlets giving the story behind each house. And food, maybe from the bygone era. And costumes! The tour guides might wear festive period clothes.

Just like that, sitting and plotting an event with her long-lost friend, Sadie feels like she never even left her old hometown.

twenty-three

For the past few days, every time the bell jangled above the general store's door, Harry glanced over to see who was coming in. Every time. A quick glance, then back to stacking sacks of ice melt. Or pointing a customer to the toasters. Or helping a shopper choose a sweatshirt. Or switching on the store's outside Christmas lights.

But when he sees the Holly Trolley parked outside the store Tuesday afternoon, and its driver, Gus Haynes, walks through the door, that's when it happens. When Harry feels his heart drop. Not only that, he also realizes it's dropped *every* time someone's walked through the general store's door since Saturday night. Since the Small Business Christmas Party.

Yes, every single time a customer's come into the store; crossed the checkerboard floor to the ornament display; or stopped at the tarnished copper trough filled with scented candles; or picked up a gift basket of candies and Bea's Brownies, his heart's dropped—sometimes just a tinge, sometimes not.

But it's been very real, that honest-to-goodness disappointment he felt every time a friend, or a neighbor, or a longtime shopper rushed in for a package of light bulbs or a ten-pound box of kindling sticks or a pair of oven mitts.

That telltale heart of his slightly ached every time the general store's bell rang over the door, and it wasn't someone in particular walking in. Someone with long blonde hair, and a fur-trimmed black parka, and a leather bag slung over her shoulder.

Every time it *wasn't* Sadie Welles—who he hasn't seen since their Saturday night dance.

"Harry!" Gus Haynes calls out now when he bustles in along with a chill breeze. His cheeks are rosy, and tufts of white hair show from beneath the tweed newsboy cap on his head. "Mighty cold out there. I think snow's a-coming."

"Gus, how you doing?" Harry asks from the soda fountain, where he just served a few hot coffees. "What can I get you today?"

"Candy canes. And lots of them."

"For the trolley?"

Gus takes a seat on a swivel stool and nods. "You bet. Every rider gets a complimentary candy cane. It's all in the Yuletide spirit."

Harry turns to the penny candy shelf and grabs two large scoops of miniature candy canes, which he pours into a paper bag. "This should do it, Gus."

"Hold your horses, fella. Add a bag of assorted penny candies, too. My grandkids will be coming by for the holiday. Need a little treat for them."

"Sure thing, Gus," Harry says while opening the jar of wrapped taffy.

"Give me some of those chocolate coins. And sugared fruit slices. Oh, and those caramel chews are great. Toss in a handful of those."

Harry looks over his shoulder and squints at Gus.

"Okay, Harry. So you caught me." Gus turns up his hands. "There never were any secrets in this here general store. The candy's for me."

"I kind of figured," Harry tells him as he lifts a scoop of the plastic-wrapped penny caramels.

"Your pop was right. He once told me that working the soda fountain was a little like being a bartender. Somehow, people's secrets always came out."

"Yep. Pop was a wise man, Gus. I miss having him around."

"I'm sure you do. Tough running the joint by your lonesome."

"My ma and sister pitch in when they can. But it's been busy, there's no denying that."

Gus gives a slow spin on his swivel stool. Harry can see that he's taking it all in—the customers in coats and scarves milling around the garland and boxed ornaments. The women with lists clutched in their gloved hands as they maneuver each crowded aisle. The line at the cash registers—where tape, gift tags and bags of bows are hung.

Finally, Gus props his elbows on the soda fountain

counter. But what he says next is *not* what Harry ever expected.

"Harry, Harry." A pause, then, "When are you ever going to marry?"

From where he dropped a scoop of gumballs into a bag, Harry looks back at Gus. "What?"

"I'm just saying … a wife might help run the store, too. Give it a woman's touch."

"Ah, jeez," Harry says while waving Gus off. "Marriage just isn't in the cards for me. Not yet, anyway."

"Maybe someday." Gus gives a wise nod. "But you're doing all right by the place for now."

As Gus says it, that disappointment-inducing bell over the door rings yet again. Harry's been let down so many times during the past few days, it's all he can do to glance over while bagging Gus' penny candy. But he does take a look, barely, then looks quickly again.

Looks quickly at Sadie Welles, who just arrived behind a teenager holding the door open for her.

Of course, how else would Harry react than to drop the candy scooper—clattering to the floor. So he picks it up, sets it aside and grabs a clean one, all while tossing another glance over his shoulder.

"Well, I'll be," Gus quietly says.

"What's that?" Harry asks as he sets two paper bags chock-full of candy on the counter.

Gus gives Harry a wink. "There really *are* no secrets in this here store."

"What are you talking about?" As Harry asks, he cuffs his flannel shirtsleeves. Well, cuffs them while glancing around the store to see just where Sadie went. He looks past two shoppers hovering near the snow shovels. Sadie's picking up an ice scraper right at that moment.

Right at the moment when Gus is watching her over *his* shoulder, too. Then he turns back to the soda fountain counter. "Someone special, Harry?"

"What?" Harry glances at Sadie, then at his watch—as though there's suddenly somewhere he has to be. "Special? Who?" he asks, straightening his watchband.

Gus says nothing. Nothing until Harry turns to him, which is when Gus raises a bushy white eyebrow before nodding toward Sadie.

"Her? No. No, Gus. She's our new tenant. Remember I told you we rented out the barn apartment?"

Gus stands then. Stands as Sadie walks straight to the soda fountain. She has on a fringed gray poncho over jeans and a black top, with a big black satchel hooked over her arm.

"Harry!" she says. "I'm glad I caught you."

"Oh, Sadie." Harry steps out from behind the counter. "Good to see you."

"You, too," she says before glancing to the Christmas décor display. "I've been meaning to ask you. Do you carry any of those tabletop ceramic Christmas trees?"

"The ones with little colored lights?"

Sadie nods—and waits—watching him.

"I think we have a few left, over in aisle—"

A sudden throat-clearing interrupts Harry, and he turns to the culprit—Gus.

"Harry? Are you going to introduce me to …" He turns to Sadie. "Sadie, is it?"

So Harry does. Names are exchanged, *Gus Haynes,*

Sadie Welles. Old friend, new tenant. Known Gus since … Sadie's in town for a new job … Harry manages to trip over his words a couple of times. Because he's onto Gus' secret shenanigans. Introductions? This is a fix-up. "Sadie's here from New Hampshire. Working as the town event planner," he lets on to Gus.

"Is that right?" Gus asks.

"I just started a few weeks ago," Sadie explains.

"And you're new to Addison?" Gus presses.

Oh, and Harry sees it. Sees the twinkle in friendly old Gus' eyes. Even in his seventies, his matchmaking tendencies still stir up in that romantic noggin of his.

"Yes. Well, no," Sadie tells him. "I mean, I lived here much of my childhood, but moved away twenty years ago. This is my first time back."

"Twenty years gone, that's a long time." Gus tips up his newsboy cap and eyes Sadie. "Now here's what I want you to do, Sadie. You take a trolley ride through town. Addison's like a winter wonderland this time of year. It's really special to see."

"Gus drives the Holly Trolley," Harry explains to Sadie. "Takes folks to Sycamore Square, or for a little sightseeing through town."

Gus turns to Harry then. "And you don't expect Sadie to ride alone now, do you? It would be nice to have someone along to point out all the decorated landmarks. And I think the gentlemanly thing to do is, well …"

And … that's it from Gus. Just a trailed-off *well,* leaving room for Harry to jump in. There's that *and* Gus' infamous raised eyebrow. Not to mention a prodding look locked onto Harry. After a few seconds, Gus ever so slightly hitches his head in the vague direction of Sadie.

Sadie, who once again is put on the spot. Put in front of an audience. First it happened with the boathouse Christmas party's kiss cam. And now, here. In front of Gus Haynes, Cupid extraordinaire—a role he's apparently got down pat.

"Sadie," Harry says, shaking his head. And recuffing a shirtsleeve. If he's not mistaken, Sadie seems to be going along with Gus. Is that a smile she's resisting while waiting for Harry to continue? Harry can't be sure, and quite frankly, he doesn't really want to put her on the spot again. "Now, about that ceramic Christmas tree you wanted. I can—"

He stops then. Stops when Gus *ahems* once more. Harry silently looks to Gus, then to Sadie—who glances from him, to Gus, then back at him.

"So anyway, Sadie," Harry says then. And pauses. And sees Gus' waiting smile. And Sadie's inquisitive expression. "Well, okay. I was wondering," Harry goes on. Another pause, and a deep breath. "Are you maybe free tomorrow night?"

❦

Riding in the green-and-gold Holly Trolley Wednesday night, Sadie feels like she's seeing every Christmas card she's ever sent. As the little streetcar sways along, those quintessential New England images swoosh past: historic homes with a candle in each window; a red countryside barn outlined with twinkly lights; white birch-log reindeer standing on front porches; an illuminated snowman wearing a jaunty top hat. There are pine wreaths on doors, garland strung around colonial lampposts.

While sitting close beside Harry, he points out the white-steepled chapel, and Whole Latte Life. Fluffy white cotton is tucked like snow into the café's window corners.

And when real snow begins to fall, don't all those tiny sparkling flakes look just like the silver glitter flecked on her Christmas cards. Why, Sadie half expects a shooting star to write out a merry greeting! Yes, if she had to say so, every holiday card she's ever sent comes to life tonight. If she had a camera, she'd take a picture of each scene and tuck the photos into a special keepsake scrapbook.

She doesn't have a camera, though. Only memory, which might be better. Already, each one is soft around the edges, nostalgic, heartwarming. A few memories in particular she'll always hold dear. The first being that Gus gave them a very personal tour of Addison—not allowing any other riders on their happy trip through town.

Another memory, well, it comes after she and Harry leave the trolley and wave goodbye to Gus in front of Dane's General Store. The long driveway to Sadie's barn apartment in the back is slippery with the snow still falling. Harry loops his arm through hers and walks her to her apartment. The night is quiet; their footsteps, muffled. They stop at her door where she left the front light on, a pretty coach light glimmering in the snow.

"Thanks, Harry," she says. "*Oh! Listen*," she whispers then. From the woodland area comes the soft *hoot-hoot* of a barred owl.

"An owl?" Harry asks.

Sadie nods, and looks at him standing there. He wears corduroy pants and a distressed leather jacket open over a cardigan sweater. A thick dark scarf is wrapped around his neck, and his brown hair is mussed from a winter breeze.

"Sounds like it's in the trees, beyond the barn," Harry tells her. His hands are tucked into his pockets; his shoulders, hunched against the cold. He gives a glance back to the general store behind them. "I've got an early day tomorrow. Setting up a North Pole mailbox station. You know, for the kids to mail their letters to Santa."

"Oh, they'll love that, Harry," she says. "Coming in with their envelopes, and … well, I had a nice time tonight, seeing Addison all decorated and festive."

Harry looks at her now. Looks at her, shifts his feet and nods. "Me, too," he says in the quiet night. "Could I have your number? Hopefully we can do something again."

Sadie can't help smiling. "Definitely."

And so right there in the snow, he programs her number into his cell phone.

Then … nothing. Just for a moment.

The moment that leads to her second dear memory.

The moment when, turning to her door, Sadie slips on an icy spot on the walkway.

Harry quickly reaches out to catch her from falling. After a *Careful, now*, he gently rights her balance. In a silent pause when Sadie steadies herself, he cups a hand to her face, leans close … and kisses her. She thinks the evening swirls with holiday magic, then, as snowflakes fall around them; as a winter wind blows her hair; as Harry reaches his other hand to cradle her face. He holds her close, kissing her longer until finally he stops, takes a breath, and tips his head to hers. His hands, they drop down behind her back. But his eyes, well, Sadie's startled to see how serious they actually are.

"Sadie," he says, his voice low.

"What is it, Harry?"

"It's just that, I wanted to tell …" he says, then takes another breath, looks away, and looks back at her. "There's something you should …" His eyes close for a second, almost as if he's trying to rid himself of some doubt. Or as if something's on his mind. "Listen, it was fun seeing the town with you tonight."

"It was."

"So, anyway. I'm not sure if you'd still … What I'm trying to say …" Harry stops, backs up a step and puts his hands in his pockets again. When the distant owl *hoot-hoots*, he looks toward the trees, then back at Sadie.

When he finally does it, finally asks her to dinner Friday night, and when Sadie nods, smiling again, he seems surprised. "Really?" he asks.

And when she assures him yes, and they agree on a time and place, he kisses her once more, quickly, before turning away toward his pickup truck parked in the store's rear lot.

Yes, if Sadie had a camera, the picture she'd snap for a scrapbook is the moment Harry looks over his hunched shoulders at her—squinting through the falling snowflakes as his feet do a little slip-slide on the slick pavement before he gives a wave.

She does the best she can, instead. She simply watches

Harry Dane get into his truck and drive off. Which is when, standing there in the cold night, Sadie closes her eyes for a few long seconds, feeling tiny snowflakes land on her face as she tucks the entire sweet memory away.

twenty-four

WHEN HARRY PUTS THE GLASS lid on his Crock-Pot Friday morning, he still can't believe it. *"Oh, it's true,"* he tells himself while setting the timer for the pot roast. Not only did he invite Sadie Welles to dinner, but he invited her to dinner at his home. She agreed, and is stopping by after she gets out of work today.

Coming by *here.*

It's the only way, and only place, to try to undo his eighteen-year mistake. If all goes well, he'll tell her about the Christmas card situation tonight. Tell her about the end table drawer filled with nearly a lifetime of her cards and messages. The talk won't be easy. But this is the only way she might understand—after a dinner when he opens his home and heart to her.

With their meal set to cook all day, Harry pulls a V-neck sweater on over his flannel, laces up his hiking boots, grabs a wool cap and heads into the store.

It's good he's working today. In between stocking shelves, and assisting customers, and placing phone orders for flashlights and snow gloves and jigsaw puzzles, he picks up some things for tonight. New candles on the dining room table would be nice, so he grabs some of those—fat pillars that'll sit on low pedestals. He hits the fudge case for a few chocolate pieces, too. And when a customer buys fringed burlap placemats with red berries and holly leaves painted in the corner, Harry snags a few for himself. All of it—the fudge, and candles, and placemats—will give the look he wants. Like he's not trying too hard. Like this all comes naturally.

Even though it doesn't. It's all just a buffer, these little extras he picks up in the store before heading home. A buffer to soften the blow, when he tries to explain the inexcusable.

⚬⚬⚬

To anyone who might look at Harry's dining room that evening, the dinner is perfect. His wood-planked table is set with those new burlap placemats. His pot roast was flawlessly slow-cooked—the meat, tender; the vegetables, dripping with gravy and flavor. Pillar candles flicker on the long table; the drum-shade chandelier casts a soft light. Hanging on the side wall, his copper pot-and-pan collection shimmers a burnished red-gold.

Yes, it all looks like the ideal dinner date. He pulls out a chair at the table for Sadie Welles. Her hair is loosely French braided, and she wears a blouse and cropped burgundy fisherman sweater over her skinny jeans. Gold earrings show beneath her hair, and a simple gold chain is looped around her neck.

"This house is as beautiful as I remember it, Harry." Sadie looks around the dining room with its low lighting, wainscoting and wide crown molding.

"From when your old neighbors lived here?" Harry returns to the kitchen then, where he spoons gravy over the pot roast platter.

"Yes. I was in this house often back then. Lorrie would watch me some afternoons when I got home from school, and my mother was working."

"Weren't you supposed to meet with Lorrie?" he calls over his shoulder. "Last week?"

"I did! She actually lives by the cove now, and we had a nice reunion on Sunday. It was really good seeing her again." Sadie turns in her seat toward the kitchen, saying, "We talked and talked, just like we did back in the day, on your porch swing."

"That's great to hear." Returning to the dining room, Harry sets the platter on the table. "And what about your job? Settling in?"

"Definitely." Sadie scoops gravy-drizzled pieces of potato onto her plate. "My office is actually in the historic Chapman Tavern."

"Right there on Main Street?" he asks while pouring their wine. "The big yellow colonial?"

"That's the place. Imagine? In the late 1700s, that very building was an actual stopover for coaches traveling between the shoreline and Hartford." She forks a piece of meat. "Can't you picture it? The spoked wheels turning on those horse-drawn buggies, with little mounted lanterns lighting the way?"

Harry nods. "Speaking of lanterns … about two dozen were delivered to the store for your Light the Night event."

"Really!" Sadie says, raising her wineglass and taking a sip. "I hope they keep coming."

"I'm sure they will." Harry raises his glass to hers. "This town goes all out for a good cause. And besides, who could say no to you?"

Sadie smiles and sets down her glass.

Perfect, right? Harry couldn't ask for a better dinner date. They dine while a cold wind rattles the windows, and candlelight flickers beside their dishes. Christmas jazz plays softly; the wine is sweet; the food, delicious.

But what anyone who might look at this scene would *not* see is this: Harry's nerves. His heart beating a little too fast. His throat feeling a little too dry. Because why, oh why did Addison's new event planner have to be … Sadie Welles? She's beautiful, and charming, and tells quirky and interesting stories—as he should've expected, based on the eighteen years' worth of Christmas cards he's read. And the thing is, he really wants to get to know her better. Maybe see a movie with her. Or ask her to Derek Cooper's Deck the Boats Festival at the cove. Have another dinner date. Dates where they'd talk, laugh, lean close as they learned more about each other.

Problem is, he already *does* know her from her Christmas card captions.

And as Harry drags a forkful of carrot and meat through dregs of gravy on his plate, he also knows he's minutes away from telling Sadie the truth. Minutes away from admitting his Christmas card blunder of the past eighteen years, then seeing where the chips might fall.

"These dishes are gorgeous, Harry," Sadie is saying now, nodding to the serving platter between them. "They look vintage?"

"They've been in the family for years," he explains around a mouthful of pot roast. "The whole collection is displayed over there." With his fork, he points to a wood hutch against the wall. Brown-and-white china pieces lean on several open shelves. Pinecones are scattered among them.

Sadie glances over her shoulder. "Oh! Do you mind?" she asks while patting a napkin to her mouth and standing. "I'd love to take a look."

When he motions for her to go ahead, she does. Her fingers drag along the vine-and-floral pattern on the edge of a dish, touch a pitcher, run around the rim of a cup and saucer, pick up a soup bowl.

"They belonged to my grandmother first, then my mother," Harry explains. "When I bought the house from my parents, they were downsizing, so the set became mine."

"You're very fortunate," Sadie tells him when she returns to the table. "To have that family history right *here* in this room … in the faded patina of this china."

"You say that like you're missing someone."

"My mother," Sadie admits. "She raised me by herself."

"Really," Harry says. He puts down his fork, pushes away his dish and doesn't say more. Doesn't say that he's aware of Sadie's family history. He knows that her mother passed away years ago, and that Sadie misses her dearly. That her tradition of sending Christmas cards is done in her memory. Instead, he stands and picks up a few plates from the table.

"Mom died when I was in college," Sadie continues. "We were so close, and sometimes it's still hard to believe she's gone."

"I hear you. Lost my pop two years ago now." Harry sets his silverware on a dish. "We used to run the store together."

"Oh, let me help." Sadie stacks a couple of dishes, too. "So you get it then," she says while breezing into the kitchen.

"Get what?"

"That Christmas isn't the same without someone you love," Sadie calls back.

Harry can only nod to that. He picks up a platter, stops and finishes his wine in a long swallow, then brings the platter and wineglass to the kitchen. On his way in, they nearly bump in the arched doorway—sidestepping this way, that way—laughing then as Sadie returns to the dining room for more dishes.

"Sadie," he says. "I've got those. Dinner was my treat. You can relax."

"I don't mind. Seriously."

When she holds out her hands for his platter, he looks at her for a long moment. Her head is tipped, her gentle hands waiting, a wisp of blonde hair fallen from her braid, her smile easy. "Okay, but just this," he says, giving her the platter.

Their hands get a little tangled up as she reaches for it. "Oops, sorry," Sadie says while fumbling with the dish.

"That's okay," Harry tells her, pointing to his cheek. "All's good, with a kiss for the cook?"

She does it—leaves a kiss on his cheek. But that's not all. Clutching the platter with one hand, Sadie touches his cheek with the other as her kiss moves to his mouth, then. A sweet kiss that he feels her smile beneath before she brushes the scruff on his jaw.

"That's better." Harry takes the platter from her. "But I'll load the dishes into the dishwasher. You get comfortable in the living room. The tree is lit, and we'll watch a Christmas movie there?"

"Okay, Harry." She squeezes his arm before heading to the living room. "That sounds really nice."

Minutes later, when Harry's filling the dishpan with soapy water, she calls out how pretty the tree looks beside the fireplace.

"I love the smell of a fresh tree," her voice carries to him. "There's something so nostalgic about it. I miss having one—even though I have my ceramic tree from your store. Don't get me wrong. *That* tree is charming, too."

"Did you find a spot for it?" Harry asks over his shoulder as he wipes off a dish and sets it in the dishwasher.

"I did. On a pedestal table. So that little tree twinkles right in the window, making the apartment festive."

She's quiet then, so Harry quickly sponges off the rest of the dishes and loads them in the dishwasher beside the sink. Afterward, he finishes wiping down the kitchen. It's all buying him time, these kitchen chores, to rehearse what he'll say to Sadie in the living room. Silently, he practices words that will tell the story of her Christmas cards—and imagines what she might say in return.

He'll say: *Sadie, there's something I have to tell you. Don't say anything until I'm done.*

184

She'll say: *Harry. You sound so serious.*

Him: *I am.*

Her: *Is everything okay?*

Him: *I really hope so, Sadie.*

Patting his forehead with the damp dishrag, he whispers a few phrases. *Didn't mean to* and *Planned to write you a note* and *Got busy* and *Thought you'd realize.*

Just then, Sadie calls out again from the living room. "What movie do you want to watch?"

"Your choice tonight, Sadie." As he dries off the Crock-Pot, Harry asks, "Have anything in mind?"

"Well, some I really love. *White Christmas* is a good one." A pause, then, "I think your remote is broken. The TV won't come on."

"Yeah, that remote's been on the fritz. Just needs batteries." Setting the Crock-Pot down, Harry gives the kitchen a once-over, then takes a long breath. "They're in the drawer, over on the side."

❧

"*In the drawer, in the drawer*," Sadie quietly says. She gives a look around the living room. Candlesticks, framed photos and hardcover books fill built-in shelves on both sides of the stone fireplace. A braided rug covers the hardwood floor; an antique-looking trunk sits in front of the sofa; a tall lamp and tarnished brass tray sit atop an old chest of drawers.

And there, near a tufted armchair, is a Queen Anne end table with one small drawer—the perfect size for batteries and such. Sadie hurries over and opens the drawer. Her hand reaches in and brushes across several Christmas cards. No batteries here. But as she starts to close the drawer, something about the top card stops her. She slowly pulls the drawer open again. That top card, with a cardinal perched on a snowcapped mailbox, catches her eye. Silently, she picks it up, then another she recognizes—its illustration a single red ornament hooked on a spindly pine tree branch. Another. Berries and greens tucked into two white ice skates hanging on a door.

"What?" she whispers, then lifts two more cards she's seen before. Santa and his reindeer fly over a wintry wonderland. A babbling brook flows beneath a snowy footbridge.

In another card, she reads a vaguely familiar greeting. And her own name. Then more cards. Penned words blur behind her sudden tears. *First snow on campus* and *I've got a dapper date* and *Missing you and Allan* and *Fluffy slippers on* and *Fondly, Sadie* and *Love, Sadie. Sadie. Sadie. Sadie.*

She'd signed every card in this very drawer. Every card she'd mailed to Lorrie and Allan for the past eighteen years? All of them? They're here. Right *here.*

There's a noise behind her. When Sadie turns—card in her hand—she sees that it's Harry. He stands there in his dark jeans and cable-knit zip-up cardigan loose over a flannel shirt. His hair is a little mussed from cleaning the kitchen; a scruff of whiskers is on his face.

And Sadie is suddenly confused about this great guy and the odd find she just stumbled across in his very home. She looks from the Christmas cards—*her* Christmas cards—and then to his concerned face. "Harry?" she asks.

twenty-five

WELL. EVERY THOUGHTFUL, CAREFUL LINE Harry Dane had rehearsed over and over just evaporated. Faded away to nothing. He stops still when he sees Sadie holding one of her very own Christmas cards. Stops still and drops his regretful eyes closed for a long moment before walking closer.

She'd opened the wrong drawer.

"Sadie," he says then. "The batteries. Well, I meant in the chest of drawers. Over there." He points to the chest with a brass tray on top of it.

"These are my cards," she whispers back, watching only him. "All of them."

"I can explain."

"So they arrived here? Every year?"

"They did. Please, Sadie. Just give me a chance to—"

Sadie opens a card she's been holding. *"Hello, Lorrie,"* she reads. *"Remember when we planned the neighborhood pet show? Well, I'm back at my alma mater, doing event planning for the college now."* After wiping a tear off her cheek, she looks up at Harry again. "These are all opened."

"They are."

"But they're addressed to Lorrie. And Allan."

"I know," Harry says, stepping closer. "But at first, I *didn't* know. I mean, I opened them the first year or two without even looking at the names on the envelope."

"What?"

"Your cards, well, they were mixed in with my family's cards. We'd just moved here," he tries to explain. "So I just opened them, and …"

Sadie walks to the sofa and sits. Sits and looks from the few cards in her hand to Harry. So Harry walks over and carefully sits beside her. Oh, there's no missing the disbelief in her eyes.

"Sadie," he says.

"These were *personal*, Harry."

Harry nods. "My mother, when your cards first arrived all those years ago, she put them in that drawer. Where you found them? And she always meant to drop you a line, I swear. But then she got busy with the store, and my father wasn't well. Things got lost in the shuffle. Or forgotten, with everything else …" Harry turns up his hands. He knows. He knows loud and clear how pathetically lame his explanation sounds.

"But your family? You all kept opening my cards?"

He shakes his head. "No, Sadie."

"But—"

"No. My family didn't. I did," Harry admits. "I opened them."

"But they were meant for Lorrie. Lorrie and Allan."

"It's just that," Harry begins. He leans his elbows on his knees, drops his head and takes a breath. When he turns and looks at Sadie beside him, he asks her a question he's often wondered. "Why did you keep sending the cards here? I mean, for all these years ... when you never heard anything back? Didn't you figure ... maybe someone moved on? Or that something happened? Or, I don't know, Sadie. But I didn't mean ..." Again, Harry looks away, then back at her. Behind her, the Christmas tree twinkles in the softly lit room. And logs are stacked in the fireplace, ready to be lit for a cozy evening. An evening when he intended to open his home and heart to Sadie Welles. Now it somehow feels that instead, everything's slipping away.

Sadie stands and walks to the Queen Anne end table, where she lifts out a few more cards. "I can't believe you've read all these. My whole life is in these cards! Private things, meant for my friends. My old neighbors." She looks over at him. "Not for you."

"I get that. It just happened, believe me. Sometimes by accident, sometimes—"

"That's actually tampering with U.S. mail. You committed a federal offense!"

"No. No, it wasn't like that. You know, in the middle of a busy day, I'd get the mail. And without even noticing the address, I'd open ... then it was too late. But they were intriguing, too."

"So for the past two weeks, at the Small Business Christmas Party, and when I'd sit at the soda fountain in your store." She squints at him then. "On the Holly

Trolley," she whispers. "You knew everything about me?"

"Not everything, no." Harry stands, turning up his hands again.

Sadie picks up another card and reads the message inside. "*I started driver's ed this fall. Maybe someday I can drive to Addison, and we'll have lemonade on your porch swing again.*"

Harry walks closer when she picks up another.

"*Merry Christmas from my dorm room!*" Sadie reads. "*Just had our first snow on campus, it's so pretty.*"

Harry walks closer still. Now, as Sadie picks another card out of the drawer, he sets his hand on her arm.

"*Sad news this Christmas, Lorrie,*" she whispers with silent tears escaping her eyes. "*We lost Mom in May. It's just not the same without her.*"

"Sadie," he says, taking the card from her and setting it on the end table. "Please, sit down. You're upset."

"Of course I'm upset. What do you *expect* me to make of all this?"

"I was going to tell you. *Here.* Tonight. Because I couldn't tell you in the store, with customers around. Or on the Holly Trolley, with Gus there."

"So all this time, though, you *knew.* You knew you had my cards, and you knew all about my personal life."

"I did, but I planned to explain, tonight, when—"

"I have to leave now." Sadie rushes to the kitchen, where her black parka is draped over a chairback.

"Sadie! Wait." When Harry gets to the kitchen, she's putting her arms in her coat sleeves and grabbing her shoulder bag off the counter. "It's not what you're thinking. I really didn't mean any harm. And I *never* imagined we'd ever actually meet."

Sadie looks long at him. "I wish we hadn't," she finally says, walking past him toward the front door.

"Wait. We can talk, please. Just let me explain."

"Explain?" Sadie asks. "You know everything about me. *Everything.*" She struggles with the front door then, twisting the knob until she finally yanks it open. "And I really know nothing about you," she whispers over her shoulder, her eyes still moist. "Not a thing."

When Sadie hurries outside to her car, she brushes against the balsam wreath hanging on his white-planked door. The battery-operated candle flickers inside the wreath's little tin house, the candle's light flashing in the house's tiny windows.

⌒⌒

Later that night, Sadie can't sleep. When she closes her eyes, all she sees are those Christmas cards in Harry Dane's end table drawer. Images swirl of snowmen and red sleighs; of candy canes and cardinals; of holly sprigs and woodland scenes. They're pieces of her whole life. So instead, she gets up and makes herself a cup of tea. Taking it to the loft, she sips the tea while looking out at the wooded thicket beyond. Moonlight falls on the trees, on the snow-dusted ground. It's a still night. Through the window, she hears the soft call of the owl. *Hoot-hoot, hoot-hoot. Hoot-hoot, hoot-hoot.* She'd once read that the barred owl's call sounds like someone asking, *Who cooks for you? Who cooks for you?*

Again the owl's call sounds in the cold, lonely night. *Hoot-hoot, hoot-hoot.*

There's no one around Sadie can talk to about Harry. No one to talk to about her lifetime of Christmas cards arriving in his mailbox each year. About him opening that mailbox and bringing her cards into his home, where he opened each and every one. She's all alone here in Addison. New to the job, only one long-lost friend to speak of. Her mother forever gone.

Hoot-hoot, hoot-hoot. Hoot-hoot, hoot-hoot.

As she looks out into the darkness, tonight it feels more like that owl is asking, *Who cares for you? Who cares for you?*

Sitting there alone and watching the night's shadows, Sadie's not sure anyone really does.

***

After seeing Sadie rush out of his house like that, now Harry's worried. He wants to be sure she made it safely back to the barn apartment. So an hour later—after an inner dialogue cursing himself for every misstep he's made with Sadie Welles—he puts on his coat and wool cap and grabs his keys. The last thing he *ever* intended was to hurt her, in any way.

Driving through Addison late at night, homes are dark now. Shadows grow long beneath the December moonlight. Tall trees silhouetted against the sky seem to mock him with a sense of foreboding. There is little traffic. All of it—the darkness, the quiet—leaves him with a sense of being completely alone. He can only imagine how Sadie feels.

When he circles The Green in his pickup, he notices

the twinkling lights kept on around the general store's front porch. Sadie's apartment is behind the store, and he glimpses her car there. For that, at least, he is thankful. She made it okay. Harry continues on, driving the empty streets alone, back home.

twenty-six

NOTHING.

That's what Harry Dane's left with after Sadie realized her cards arrived *exactly* where she'd sent them for the past eighteen winters. Arrived at an olive-green Craftsman bungalow next door to her old home.

Since their dinner fell apart, nothing from Sadie. Not in four days. It's Tuesday, with no Sadie breezing into the store for a package of paper plates, or a candle for her table. No Sadie sitting at the soda fountain asking for a coffee to go, and chatting while she waits. Sure, he could call or text her, but now it just doesn't feel right.

And with Christmas fast approaching, they're both really busy. So there's been nothing between them except uncomfortable nods and brief waves. Even those only happened a few times—when Harry pulled his truck into the store's rear parking lot each morning as Sadie drove out to work. And there was the incident at the gas station, too. Harry stood there filling his tank, not realizing Sadie stood at the next pump over until it was too late. Until she hurried into her car without looking his way, then drove off before he had a chance to say hello. A chance to try to patch things between them. Maybe crack a lame joke. Or comment on the snowstorm predicted this week. Something.

No, what Harry has instead is lanterns.

Lantern deliveries from every small business in town don't stop. Tall and small, bronze and tin. Black, silver and red. Farmhouse style and contemporary. Hanging lanterns and standing. Rustic wood and elaborate scrolled metals. Lanterns fill the rear stockroom of Dane's General Store, and fill part of the store's cargo van, too. Sadie's Light the Night event is a hit already—before it's even begun.

But Harry can't tell her that. Instead, the last thing he sees when he closes up the store each night is her ceramic Christmas tree illuminated in the apartment window. And he remembers her last words to him. *I really know nothing about you. Not a thing.*

But she does. Sadie knows one thing—all her Christmas cards are in his end table drawer. And that bothers him enough to keep him up at night. To have him pace in his robe and slippers at home; get a drink of water; look out his windows onto the dark night.

Until he remembers something his father often told him. *Do what's right, Harry,* Pop would say whenever Harry got himself into a predicament. Whenever his conscience was challenged. *Do what's right, and you'll sleep well at night.*

So after another restless night, one when his pop's

words echoed in his mind, Harry does it. He does the right thing. Early Tuesday morning, he makes a phone call and delivers eighteen winters' worth of Christmas cards to their rightful owner.

⁓

"Harry?" a woman asks when she opens the ranch house's front door.

"Yes. Harry Dane," he says to the woman. Her silvery blonde hair is side-parted and shoulder length. Wire-framed eyeglasses give her a mod look. And her smile is instant. "You must be Lorrie."

"I am! And I'm *so* glad you called." She opens the door further. "Please. Do come in."

Right away, Harry can see why Sadie continued sending cards to Lorrie all these years. Lorrie has a way about her that puts you at ease.

"Don't mind Buster," she says over her shoulder while walking through the house. "I adopted him from the shelter a few months ago, and he's never left my side."

"Buster." Harry bends and gives a pat to the small Sheltie mix tiptoeing around his feet. "You look like a good dog."

"He is," Lorrie says. "Buster keeps me company when we take walks by the cove. *Come here, boy,*" she calls to Buster now. She and the dog lead Harry into the dining room. Iced raspberry pastry is set out on a large table, along with a tarnished-silver coffee carafe near two mismatched china cups. There's also a dog biscuit on a plate, over on the side. Lorrie points Buster to a round dog bed in the corner, gives him the biscuit, then sits and motions to Harry. "We'll chat with our coffee. Have a seat, Harry."

He does. Harry pulls out a chair and sits, too. He also puts the bag he'd brought along on the dining room table. The room's large windows let in the morning sunshine. In its light, the dulled silver carafe glimmers. China plates stacked and lined up on a mahogany sideboard look even more aged beneath the rays of sun catching swirling dust particles.

Just then, the back door opens and Lorrie turns in her seat. "Oh, Allan! Come in here, I want you to meet Harry Dane."

A tall man wearing a fleece jacket and earmuffs walks in with an armload of split logs. "Harry," he says with a nod toward his filled hands. "I'd shake, but you don't want a splinter."

"That's okay." Harry gives a wave across the room. "Good to meet you, Allan."

"I must tell you …" Lorrie cuts in. "My husband and I have been to your store a few times since we moved back to Addison." As she says it, Lorrie stands, lifts the carafe and fills their coffee cups.

"What a terrific spot that general store is," Allan adds on his way to the living room. "But I'm off," he calls back while dropping his logs near the fireplace. "Got a woodpile that needs some tending."

"Take care, Allan," Harry calls with another wave.

"You too, Harry." Allan nods and heads through to the kitchen.

"Just be careful out there, Al. And don't forget to wear

197

those new work gloves," Lorrie reminds him as he's out the door.

"It's a cold one today. Good day to keep the fire stoked," Harry says with a glance toward a back window.

"Don't you sell kindling at your store?" Lorrie asks, sitting again at the table.

"Sure do. Ten-pound boxes."

"A true country store. Got a bit of everything at Dane's, don't you?"

"We try, Lorrie. My folks bought the place when I was in college," Harry tells her while reaching for his steaming cup of coffee. "I've taken over running the store the past few years now."

"You know, my friend Sadie stopped by for a visit the other day. And she mentioned that she was renting the barn apartment *behind* your store, Harry."

"That's right," Harry says while clearing his throat.

"And Sadie says her apartment's a lovely place, too. Very, how did she put it, rustic chic?"

"Sadie. Like I mentioned on the phone, Sadie's why I'm here today."

"She's okay?"

"Yes. Yes, she's fine. It's just that, well, we've been seeing each other here and there. And the other night, Lorrie, she mentioned her visit with you. That you did a lot of catching up."

"Did we ever." Lorrie stirs cream into her coffee. "Especially after losing touch for such a long time."

"So I was wondering ..." Harry pauses as Lorrie sets a piece of pastry on each of their plates. "When you saw her, did she happen to mention the Christmas cards she'd sent you all these years?"

"She did! Said she never stopped sending them, either, and was surprised to know I never got them."

"Well, Lorrie." Harry lifts his coffee cup, but sets it back down. Sets it down and gives a regretful smile. "I actually have your cards here with me, today."

⁓

It feels a little bit like confession.

Harry chooses his words carefully as he does the right thing. As he tells Lorrie the story behind eighteen years of Christmas cards. And he doesn't mince those words when he says that at first, the cards were opened inadvertently. And that his mother had good intentions to contact Sadie, but never followed through. Life, well it pulled no punches with his mother—first with managing a busy general store, then with his father's heart surgery and recuperation. Through it all, Sadie's cards came. Through Harry buying the Craftsman bungalow from his parents, and assuming responsibility for those cards then, too. Through relationships, and deaths, and snowstorms, and funny fiascos of Christmas kittens and spilled jam jars, always … always there was an unexpected card from Sadie. Harry thought that she'd eventually catch on and stop sending them, but they kept coming.

"And then, of course, Sadie walked into the general store with a suitcase in hand—which just about floored me," Harry says. "Long story short? It all led to this moment now, talking to you."

"Oh, life has a funny way of circling around us, doesn't it?"

199

"It was still wrong of me to keep opening her cards, Lorrie. I'm deeply sorry and apologize for doing so." He reaches into the bag beside him and pulls out eighteen cards. The envelopes are of all shapes and sizes and colors. Some of the cards' illustrations are visible beneath the ripped envelope flaps. Glimpses of ornaments and Santas and cardinals show through.

"You kept them? All of them?" Lorrie asks.

"I did. In an end table drawer in my living room. I'm not sure why, but I did." Harry glances at a few of the envelopes. "Sometimes there was something sad in Sadie's words. I don't know. Maybe sometimes I even hoped things would work out for her. So I put them in the drawer, thinking that after the holidays, I'd drop her a line telling her that you'd moved away."

"And that never happened?"

Harry shakes his head. "When I closed that drawer every December, the cards were only a passing thought until the next December, when another would arrive. And now, all these years later, well I hope it's not too late to do the right thing."

"It's *never* too late to do the right thing," Lorrie says.

"In that case ..." Harry slides the pile of cards across the table. "I think these are yours."

The room goes silent then. Lorrie takes the cards and gently pulls one from an envelope. "*Merry Christmas from my first apartment,*" she whispers. Then, "*Sad news this Christmas. We lost Mom in May.*" And, "*Don't mind the powdered sugar and green sprinkles on the card.*"

After that? Nothing. Lorrie says no more words. But she continues looking at the cards, one at a time. When she's gone through about ten of them, she stops. Stops and collects the cards together in one stack. Harry's not sure what to make of it all, except that maybe she's overcome with emotion. But apparently, she's not.

"I think you're wrong, Mr. Dane."

"Pardon me?"

Lorrie sets the cards back on his side of the table. "These are not mine."

"I don't understand."

She takes a sip of her coffee, then sets the cup in its saucer. There's only the clink of the china followed by a quiet moment. Finally, Lorrie says, "If I'd *only* read those cards, then yes. I'd think they were mine. But ... I also watched you tell me your story. A very personal, and moving, story. I heard your voice. The care in your words. And I see your face. Your concerned eyes. Those cards, each and every one of them, arrived *exactly* where they needed to arrive. And were opened by *exactly* who needed to open them."

When she sweeps her hand toward him to take the cards, Harry does. Cautiously. And when she nods at him, he lifts one, opens it and silently reads Sadie's words. Something about staying in New Hampshire, and a new job. He sets the card down, looks to Lorrie, then lifts another card—as though there's some answer he missed inside it. *Quiet Christmas this year.* And another, then another. *Missing you. All my love. Sadie. Sadie. Sadie.*

"If you want to do the right thing, Harry, well ..." Lorrie gives him a kind smile, reaches across the table and squeezes his hand. "I think you came to the wrong place."

twenty-seven

THREE SMALL WORDS STAY WITH Harry—Lorrie's words to him yesterday, suggesting he'd come to the wrong place to make amends.

The wrong place.

Because Harry knows the right place. Knows where he has to go: Sadie's doorstep. Problem is, when? And how?

By Wednesday afternoon—one week before Christmas—problem solved. A snowstorm had been predicted for several days. So when the snow begins lightly falling, he sends his sister, Emma, home and closes up the general store early. The roads will soon be slick, and it's safest for everyone to stay off them.

Everyone except Harry. He figures he can now get to that *right place* before the storm hits full force.

Can still right an eighteen-year wrong.

So he starts planning while driving home; while squinting out past his swishing windshield wipers; while snow dusts lawns and porches and lampposts. To get what he needs, though, a quick stop at Emma's house comes first. Which isn't easy, with the way he has to brush off curious questions from his sister and mother.

"Really? You need my old movie projector?" his mother asks.

"And the portable screen," Harry tells her. "Where is it?"

"In the hall closet, but—"

"Got it," Harry says as he pulls the rolled-up screen from a corner in the front coat closet.

"You're going to watch our home movies?" Emma asks, following him to the door. "*Tonight?*"

"Long story," he says while flipping up his coat collar against the snow, then heading back out to his truck. *Eighteen years long*, he thinks.

⁓

When there's a knock at her door that evening, Sadie's not really surprised to open it and see Harry Dane standing there in the falling snow. His collar's flipped up on the wool peacoat he wears, and snowflakes dust the dark cap on his head.

"Sadie," he says.

"Harry?" She briefly glances past him. "What are you doing here?"

"Can I come in?"

She looks closely at him and sees some type of duffel and gear slung over his shoulder.

"It's important, Sadie."

"Yes. Of course," she tells him while opening the door further. Just then, a cold wind gusts. Tiny snowflakes reaching her face feel like icy pinpricks.

Harry stamps the snow off his trail boots and walks in. He hesitates for only a moment, then continues straight into her living room, where barnwood beams cross the vaulted ceiling and logs burn in the fireplace and a fringed throw is tossed over the couch. Sadie was just about to settle in for a cozy evening at home—maybe put on her robe and fluffy slippers, then make some hot cocoa while the snow falls outside.

Instead, she watches as Harry looks around, sets down his duffel and pulls something out of a carrying case. Walking across the room, he finally opens what looks like metal tripod legs on some contraption he brought. Then he pulls up a … movie screen?

"Harry?" Sadie asks. "What are you doing?"

Harry stops then. Stops and grabs off his wool cap, which he tucks into his coat pocket before running a hand through his dark, tousled hair. Only then does he look at her. Directly. There's a long, quiet moment before he talks. Even then, he doesn't say much. But it's enough.

"I'm really sorry, Sadie, about the other night. When you found your cards after dinner. I *never* meant to hurt you like that, and hope you can forgive me. I did something wrong for eighteen years—opening those Christmas cards—and want to make things right. Between us. But I didn't know how. Until now."

"I don't understand." Sadie stands there, arms crossed in front of her. "What does this movie screen have to do with it all?"

"Everything." Harry takes off his peacoat and hangs it over the back of a chair. "When you were at my house the other night, you were upset when you left—and with good reason. I had a secret window into your life for a long time. And when you walked out after dinner, the last thing you said was that I knew everything about you, and, well, you knew nothing about me."

"Harry."

"No, it's true, Sadie. You *don't* know anything about me. Not much, anyway." He unzips the duffel at his feet and pulls out an old, cumbersome movie projector. "And tonight? I'd like to change that."

∽◯

Harry has nothing to lose. The last few days were filled with such remorse, such regret, he couldn't feel any lower. But with a shred of hope, he sets the projector on an end table and aligns the table with the movie screen before glancing at Sadie. She wears a loosely tucked, cream-colored sweater over cropped black jeans. Her wide leather belt has a burnished-gold buckle; her ankle boots are suede.

And her voice, soft. Especially when she asks, "Are these old home movies?"

Harry nods, then attaches a film reel on the projector and threads the film through the gears. "My mother, well, she's into vintage. I mean, seriously. Thus buying an old-fashioned general store with my father years ago. *And* the Craftsman house. All good stuff, all vintage. And all my life," he continues as he motions for Sadie to sit on the sofa, "she used an old 8mm camera for any home movies she took." He attaches an empty reel to the projector and feeds the film into a slot then, saying over his shoulder, "She said this is how home movies should be. Silent. Watched in darkness. And I guess she's right. The scenes are a little more vague this way, like memories are."

He says nothing more. Neither does Sadie, he notices. Instead, she quietly curls up on the sofa and pulls a plaid throw over her lap as he tinkers with the projector controls. "Can you switch off the lights?" he asks when he finally turns on the projector motor and gets the reels turning. The projector hums, those reels click, and in the darkness, Harry Dane shows Sadie Welles his life.

twenty-eight

FOR THE NEXT HOUR AND a half, they don't say a lot. The silent home movies pretty much speak for themselves as the film reels click and the projector lighting flickers. Together, he and Sadie watch a few of his childhood Christmases and birthdays in the family's old colonial. Candles are blown out on cakes; tinsel glimmers on Christmas trees. Seasons change. Eight-year-old Harry jumps into ocean waves on a hot summer day; ten-year-old Emma sits out in the yard with their golden retriever. Sunshine glares into the camera as bicycles are pedaled. Snowbanks heap along sidewalks while snow forts are built. The movies are choppy. And the colors? They're faded on the decades-old footage, such that the scenes could portray any typical Addison family—their life caught in visual snippets.

When the Craftsman bungalow comes on the screen, Harry says a few words. It's the more recent years that he feels need explanation. Maybe because those are the years that coincide with Sadie's holiday cards landing in his mailbox.

My parents bought the house when I was in college.
Me and Pop hanging the new store sign.
Christmas kittens.
Broken wrist, after stealing the store van. Foolish kids.
College girlfriend, Tess, at my twenty-first birthday.
Washing new truck in driveway, the year I moved back home.
Sanding and painting front door on bungalow, after I bought the house.
The year I saved Christmas, at the bungled tree-lighting ceremony.

But when the final scene begins, capturing the day that Dane's General Store won the Window Wonderland competition, Harry gets up and stops the projector, mid-scene.

"Harry?" Sadie looks over at him from the sofa. She had slipped off her ankle boots and now draws her knees up.

"There you have it," he says, standing in the dark living room of the barn apartment. "My life. All of it."

"But ..." She looks from him, to the stalled image on the movie screen. "There's more."

Harry remembers the moment frozen on the screen. It's a shot of the general store when the town declared Dane's had the best winter window display. Twinkling white lights frame the storefront, and snow dusts the windowpanes—behind which the store's model train chugs past bottle-brush trees and through the ceramic village set in tufts of cotton. On that day, he'd also just come off the hardest year of his life—after unexpectedly losing his father.

And now? Now Harry's not sure what does it: that thought alone, or the unveiling of his *entire* ordinary life, tonight, to Sadie Welles. Either way, he's pretty much choked up and has to look away. Drag a hand through his hair. Take a long breath.

Finally, he looks at Sadie. She's still watching him from the sofa. The only light in the room comes from her ceramic Christmas tree in the window and the flames crackling in the fireplace. Painfully apparent, also, is the single beam of light from the idled movie projector. Okay, so if Harry's going to make things right, there's only one way. He can't hold back on *any* of his life.

"That," he begins then, nodding to the decorated storefront, "came at the end of the worst year of my life, Sadie."

She looks to the movie screen, then back to him.

"I lost my father the winter before, and it pretty much derailed me. Pop and I were really close. And I didn't know if I could keep the store going without him, once he died."

"But you did," she whispers.

Harry starts to talk, but stops after a word or two and just walks back to the couch. He sits beside her, elbows on his knees, and looks at Dane's General Store in full living color on that portable screen. There's the store sign hung over the dark brown porch; the wreath on the entrance door; the decorated tree standing in a banded wooden barrel; the decked-out store windows outlined in white lights. He looks for a long second before dropping his head. In a moment, he feels Sadie's light touch on his shoulder.

"Harry," she whispers. "Tell me about the store."

When he looks at her, he hesitates. Sadie leans close beside him, her knees curled beneath her. "I messed up," he finally says.

"With the store?"

"No." He drags both hands through his hair. "With you. Every year, I'd open those cards and put them in that drawer thinking that you'd eventually catch on and stop sending them. Or that maybe I'd write you a note. Something. But once I closed that drawer, I got busy and really didn't think of the cards again until the next one arrived a year later. None of it was intentional. It was just … your cards came in and out of my life like that." He motions to the stilled store image on the movie screen. "In and out of *that* life."

"Oh, Harry," Sadie says, her voice soft.

When he looks at her beside him on the sofa again, her eyes are filled with tears. But her look is gentle now. There's no suspicion, no anger there. So he turns and faces her. Tips his head. Touches her hair. "I opened your cards. I just did. In all *those* years, while I was living *those* days," he says, nodding to the portable screen. "Yes, I committed a federal offense," he tells her, his voice low as he takes her face in his hands, leans in and whispers, "So sue me, Sadie."

❧

Harry kisses her then, and when his lips touch hers, Sadie slightly—just slightly—sobs. Oh, life is cruel sometimes. It takes us in roundabout directions that hide where it's really leading us. During the past few days, she'd gone from feeling optimistic and buoyant to hurt and uncertain—until finally ending up in this unexpected and emotional moment. Her hopes and doubts have swirled like the swirling snow falling outside. Tiny ice crystals tap the windows now. Sadie hears the blowing wind as Harry holds her face and kisses her.

And she kisses him back—slowly at first. When he pulls away and starts to whisper something, she shakes her head, no. This time, it's *her* hands that rise to his face, that touch the scruff of whiskers on his jaw as she kisses him again. This time, the kiss is more. This time, it's like one long inhale, necessary to live. Her hands, they touch his neck, and move behind him as he kisses her still, all while she leans back on the sofa.

But Harry stops then. Stops, touches a fallen wisp of her hair and whispers, "Wait."

Sadie does. She waits as Harry gets up and snaps off that movie projector. The room's darker now. Only that ceramic Christmas tree glimmers near the window, and low flames flicker around the logs in the fireplace. So she and Harry move in dark shadow when he sits with her. And touches her neck. And kisses her lips lightly once, then again.

Somehow, with icy snowflakes tapping the windows, the evening becomes more about whispers than talking. Whispered assurances. *It's okay*, and *I'm so glad you're back in Addison*. Whispered affections. *You're very beautiful*, and

I wanted so badly to see you again. And when he tugs her sweater up from her jeans, she stops him with one more whisper. *Come with me.*

⁓

In Sadie's bedroom, the night changes. When she leads him through the doorway, Harry takes in the pitched barnboard ceiling; the cream-painted planked walls. The golden light from the lamp on her bedside table. He sees it all. The dried wreath hanging from an antique window shutter on the far wall. The basket collection on top of a painted dresser. Tucked in the corner near her bed, a decorative floor-to-ceiling tree branch wrapped in tiny white lights.

Sadie.

Sadie stopped beside him in her cream sweater, black jeans, stockinged feet.

Sadie watching him.

What happens next is like much of what's happened over the past eighteen years. The night becomes one Harry will remember in bits and moments, just like the sparse lines in eighteen years of Christmas cards. Sparse lines, sparse moments that say everything.

Him lifting off her sweater; she slipping off his flannel shirt and dropping it on the foot of the bed. Her hands gently reaching around him when he bends and kisses her. For every move he makes, so does she. More moments. Undressing each other, the slight touches as they do. Icy snow crystals tapping at the windowpane. Murmurs beneath the patchwork quilt on her bed. Harry lying

212

beside her, pressing his lips to her shoulder, down to the soft of her throat. The glimmer of light from the illuminated branchlets close by. The sensation of her mouth, her fingers on his skin. Sadie beneath him. His hand tracing the curve of her hip. The wind whistling outside. Sadie whispering his name.

twenty-nine

A NOISE WAKES HARRY EARLY the next morning. But he doesn't open his eyes. No, no, no. If he keeps his eyes closed, he won't have to see reality. Won't have to admit that the night before was only a dream, and that he's really in his own bedroom in his Craftsman bungalow.

With his eyes closed, he can believe he's somewhere else.

But that noise, growing louder—over and over— finally gives it away. A heavy scraping noise, and a truck engine. Okay, so it's the snowplow outside—which can mean only one thing.

No, Harry's not at home. Not in his own bedroom.

Yes, he's *really* in the barn apartment behind Dane's General Store, and that snowplow is going to be Derek's, clearing the store's rear parking lot. He does that for local small businesses.

So Harry opens his eyes and turns his head. The lights

still twinkle on the tall branch in the corner. And Sadie lies beside him. She's wearing his flannel shirt and seems to still be asleep. He waits a minute, then almost reaches to touch her beautiful mussed hair, but stops himself. Because does Sadie truly want him here this morning? Did she really understand his life story last night? Or did they just get caught up in a snowy, Christmastime moment that landed them in her bedroom? So instead, he looks toward the window, but the curtains are drawn and he can't tell if it's still snowing outside. When he lifts his watch from the bedside table to check the time, it doesn't really matter if it's snowing. What matters is that it's late, and he has to get to the store to shovel the front walkway.

And he needs his flannel shirt to do that.

"Sadie," he whispers.

All the while, as Sadie wakes up, and gently touches his jaw; as she quickly gets on her clothes so that she can give him his shirt; as he gets dressed while Sadie heads to the kitchen; as he declines her offer of breakfast; as he puts on his peacoat in the living room, the questions in his mind begin. Was this all a mistake? "*No, not for me,*" he whispers. Does Sadie want him here like this? *I hope so*, he thinks. Is her offer of breakfast just a formality? Glancing back toward where she fusses with cupboards and dishes, the only answer he can come up with is, *I don't know*.

He feels better about things, though, when her voice calls from the kitchen. "Wait!"

Harry turns as he's pulling on his wool cap. Sadie, in her jeans and sweater, rushes over with a thermos of hot coffee.

"You know," she says. "To sip while you clear the

snow, and open up your store."

"Thanks, Sadie," he tells her, taking the thermos. He turns to go outside, but turns back to her, first. Turns back and takes a step closer. "Last night—"

"Was perfect," she finishes for him.

He nods, and tugs down his hat. "It was," he says while hearing Derek's plow moving around snow outside. "And I'll come back later, to pick up the movie projector?"

She nods, too. Just nods, with a hesitant smile.

"Okay, then. Well, I better get to work," he begins, then looks at his thermos and back to her. And steps even closer. When he leans down to give her a kiss, they get a little tangled up as he reaches around her with the thermos in hand. A bump, a scoot to the side, and a quick kiss, then another, and he's out the door.

⁂

Out the door and under instant scrutiny as Derek Cooper stops plowing and waves Harry over.

"I'll give you a hand with the snow," Harry calls out as he crosses the slippery parking lot.

"You living *there* now?" Derek asks through the open driver's window of his pickup. He points to the barn apartment.

"What?" Harry looks over his shoulder.

"I thought you rented out the place."

"Yeah. Yeah, we did." Harry glances back at the barn again. "Had to fix something. On the stove. The pilot light, you know," Harry bluffs as he keeps walking past Derek toward the store's rear entrance.

216

The rear entrance still completely locked up.

The rear entrance where his own pickup is buried beneath six inches of fresh-fallen snow after being parked there all night.

When he gets to the store's door, he turns to face Derek in his still-idled truck. "I'll just open up and get started clearing the front," Harry calls back to him.

Derek says nothing. Just raises an eyebrow, nods, and begins plowing another swath of snow.

⁓

With much Light the Night planning to be done, Sadie knows she'll be working late today. Her itinerary is growing, including managing the lanterns. They keep arriving at Dane's drop-off for her big event on Christmas Eve—which is already next week! So since she's not sure what time she'll be home, Sadie carefully packs up Harry's movie projector and portable screen. It's easy enough to bring them back to him on her way to work. That, and it gives her a reason to see him again. When she walks in the store an hour later, Harry excuses himself from a customer and hurries over.

"Sadie. Everything okay?"

Sadie nods. "Yes, it's just that ..." She lifts his home movie gear and tries to explain how she doesn't know what time she'll be home. Somehow then, between his *Oh, okay*, and her *I didn't want you to think*, and his *No problem*, and her *I really had a nice time, but have to run*, and his *Sure, Sadie, I understand*, he manages to take the gear from her—reaching one hand as she reaches her other and they get tangled up again before finally disentangling with a flustered laugh. In a store that's gone quiet. A store filled with customers stealing a furtive glance at them. Right until Sadie nods, turns and quickly walks back out to her car.

The awkwardness of their encounters today—both first thing in her apartment, and afterward in the store—stays with Sadie. And it has her worry at times, when she wonders if their unease means maybe the whole situation just won't work. But at other times, she smiles, thinking of the charm of it all—the serendipity—and she feels hopeful.

Like later that evening. While her dinner's simmering inside on the stove, she grabs a broom and steps out her front door. The night is cold, and wispy clouds pass by a sliver of moon. Wearing her black parka and mittens, Sadie sweeps new snow flurries off the barn apartment's stoop, then sweeps off the antique milk can there, too. All the while, a soft sound comes to her. It's the muted call of the barred owl, from somewhere in the snowy woods. *Hoot-hoot. Hoot-hoot. Hoot-hoot. Hoot-hoot.*

Who cares for you? Sadie hears in the owl's echo.

She glances over to Dane's General Store across the small parking lot. The store's open late tonight and is all lit up. Twinkly lights outline even the rear window. The parking lot is filled with shoppers' cars. Harry's pickup truck is there, too.

Who cares for you? the owl seems to call again.

Sadie leans on the broom and squints through the evening light. Maybe … just maybe it's been Harry Dane all along.

thirty

BY LATE FRIDAY AFTERNOON, LAST-MINUTE details for the Light the Night event keep Sadie busy at work. That's where she's been holed up, in her office in the historic Chapman Tavern. The pale yellow colonial-turned-office-building looks out on Main Street, where holiday shoppers rush from store to store. In between phone calls to vendors for her event, Sadie wistfully looks out the paned window near her desk. Storefronts are twinkling; snowflakes drift down in a light flurry; the Holly Trolley jingles past.

But instead of being out there in the holiday bustle, she focuses on the task at hand. Printed diagrams and illustrations of Addison's town green cover her desk. Every angle is considered. More photographs showing The Green from the east side, west side, and even from an aerial drone-view fill her computer screen. And on each sketch, each photo, Sadie has noted the places that will hold the unending lanterns donated by town businesses. There will be lanterns lining the low stone wall surrounding the wishing fountain; lanterns in the banded wooden flower barrels dotting The Green; lanterns surrounding coach-light lampposts; lanterns hanging from low tree branches. Finally, a small, portable bleacher section will be delivered and set up where the towering town Christmas tree *used* to be—before being struck by lightning. Every seat on the bleachers will be filled, end to end, with illuminated lanterns.

And every hour of her weekend will be filled, too. She and her assistant will be stationed at The Green, marking out and roping off lantern locations.

When Sadie hears her coworkers closing up their offices and chatting about the holiday, she checks her watch. One last review of her Light the Night itinerary, and she'll be good to go, too. At the very least, being incredibly busy with work has distracted her from, well, from one thought that's wanted to plant itself in her mind.

From Harry Dane.

From Harry Dane, who she hasn't said more than a passing greeting to since he spent Wednesday night with her. Since he presented his entire life in silent 8mm film. There's been only a wave as she drove past him going to work, right as he pulled into the general store's parking lot. And there was a quick hand clasp with a *Good to see you, Sadie* when she stopped in the store this afternoon for a take-out coffee. She saw, then, how busy the store was, and how many customers needed Harry's attention just days before Christmas.

So the distraction of her own work has distracted her

from her worries—her thoughts of Harry and what their snowy night together meant.

"*And there you go*," she whispers when her cell phone rings this time, distracting her once again. "Sadie here," she answers.

"Sadie! It's Lorrie."

"Lorrie? How nice to hear from you."

"I'm so glad I caught you, dear. I have a bit more Christmas shopping to do, and would *love* to have some company. Are you free?"

"Seriously?" Sadie looks out her window at the shoppers she's envied all week. "When?"

"Now?"

After one glance over at her coworkers putting on their coats and mittens, and a glance at her flickering computer screen, then another out her office window to the snowy, twinkling scene outside, Sadie tells Lorrie that right now would be perfect. "I'm about to clock out. We're closing up here until after the holiday. Can you meet me outside the old Chapman Tavern on Main?"

Right as she finishes talking to Lorrie, the office staff gathers near Sadie's doorway. Amidst their *See you at Light the Night*, and *Have a merry Christmas*, Sadie shuts off her computer, lifts her camel coat off the hook on her office door, and grabs up a pile of folders stuffed with Light the Night paperwork.

"Oh, before you go!" her assistant, Bev, says. "Even though I'm helping you set up this weekend, we got you a little something for now."

"That's so nice of you," Sadie manages while slipping into her coat. "You *shouldn't* have."

221

"But it was fun! We all wanted to welcome you to your job here with a Christmas token, that's all." Bev sets a green-and-gold gift bag on Sadie's desk.

Distractions or not, there's no escaping thoughts of Harry—no matter which way Sadie turns. She's reminded of him even as she reaches into the ribboned bag and pulls out the gift from her coworkers. It's a large, hand-painted Christmas ornament depicting the town she's falling in love with—Addison. As she thanks her new office friends for thinking of her, she looks closely at the painted scene-on-glass. There, among the colonial homes and coffee shop and boutiques and steepled church and town green, she sees it. Can't miss the dark brown, farmhouse-style building with its twinkling lights wrapped around the porch posts. Ever so lightly then, she brushes a finger over the painted rendering of Dane's General Store.

⁓

Two hours later, Sadie and Lorrie sip cinnamon dolce lattes while sitting in a windowside booth at Whole Latte Life. Tufts of white cotton are tucked along the windowsill; their hats and gloves are tucked on the seat beside them; their shopping bags are tucked on the floor. Sadie just told Lorrie that she and her assistant, Bev, will be working around the clock on The Green this weekend. Light the Night is just days away, and there are lantern locations to be roped off; crowd control to be discussed with authorities; food vendors to be directed; donation tables to be delivered.

Now, though, she wants to talk about something else.

About *someone* else. So she tells Lorrie about Harry—and how she's not sure what to make of him.

"He came to see me," Lorrie confides.

"Harry did?" Sadie asks. "He went to your house?"

"Yes. He stopped by a few days ago." Lorrie sips from her steaming drink. "He said he wanted to right a wrong, and tried to return all your Christmas cards to me."

"Tried?" Sadie asks. "What do you mean, *tried?*"

"Harry apologized, Sadie. Said how sorry he was for opening eighteen years' worth of Christmas cards meant for me and Allan. He just never thought it would come to this. But," Lorrie says as she reaches across the booth and gives Sadie's hand a squeeze. "I didn't accept the cards."

"You didn't?"

Lorrie shakes her head. "Instead, I bundled them together, slid them to him across my dining room table and told him that if he wanted to right a wrong, I believed he'd come to the wrong place."

"Oh, Lorrie." Sadie glances out the coffee café's window onto The Green across the street. Balsam wreaths hang on lampposts there. Tiny white lights are strung up surrounding trees from which Sadie's lanterns will hang. So much has happened in the few weeks since she's moved back to Addison. She started her new job, and reconnected with Lorrie, and moved into her apartment. And met Harry.

She tells Lorrie now how Harry came over with a lifetime of home movies for her to watch. It was the only way he knew how to explain his whole life, *and* how her Christmas cards came into that life. She also says that she isn't sure if the night backfired, because she hasn't heard much from Harry since then.

"Was he embarrassed by showing me the movies?" Sadie asks. "Did he really want me to see his entire life? A beautiful life … that it is, Lorrie. But I can't read him, and haven't seen much of him since then."

"Have you talked at all?"

"No. We've both been so busy—me planning Light the Night, him at the store. We just briefly pass each other with a friendly greeting."

"But what about in here?" Lorrie asks, patting her heart. "What do you feel there?"

"Meeting Harry the way I did, and finding all my cards at his house? I don't know, Lorrie," Sadie says, then sips her latte. "It's either the most amazing story, or it's the saddest I've known."

"Sadie." Lorrie gives her a gentle, warm smile.

And somewhere in that smile, doesn't Sadie see her own mother? In Lorrie's voice, doesn't she hear some inflection of her mother's, too? Sadie briefly closes her eyes against sudden tears, all while listening to the soft words meant only for her.

"Christmas is about believing," Lorrie tells her, leaning close over the table. "And you, dear Sadie, need to believe in the best of Harry Dane."

❧

Well, if there's one place all about believing, it's Snowflakes and Coffee Cakes—the grand Christmas shoppe and bakery on the cove. Sadie and Lorrie make one more shopping stop there. Inside, the spirit of Christmas hangs from every rafter in glittering, dangling snowflakes. Mechanical carolers dressed in fur-lined cloaks, and scarves, and tweed topcoats raise their heads in song. Swags of green garland drape from every shelf and banister; candles flicker in each window; a sparkling swan carousel spins 'round and 'round. Up in the loft, a Christmas train chugs through valleys, and hills of pine, and around log cabins in an immense snow village. In the back of the store, the candy-cane alley is like a funhouse for old and young alike. Then there are baskets of vintage ornaments and boxes of old Christmas records. In the middle of it all, a twelve-foot fresh-cut balsam tree looks nearly silver beneath the delicate tinsel strung from every branch.

Filled with awe while crossing the wood floor, Sadie hopes for one thing: to find just the right Christmas present for the last person on her list. For Harry Dane. Something that says she believes.

❧

Later, back in her barn apartment, Sadie sets out a small box and wrapping paper. Carefully, she picks up the gift she'd finally found for Harry at the Christmas shoppe. The item was on the Near and Deer table display of carved woodland animals. Most of the carvings were of deer, with smaller whittled animals tucked among them.

Sadie picks up the wooden owl now. Its every feather is detailed; its expression, wise. The carving is mounted on an actual piece of tree branch. When she saw it, one question came to mind. *Hoot-hoot. Hoot-hoot.* "Who cares for you?" she whispers while wrapping the owl in tissue paper and setting it in the gift box.

Yes, Sadie knows the answer. She does believe.

thirty-one

ALL DAY SATURDAY, THE GENERAL store is mobbed. Parents and children wait in line outside to drop their letters to Santa in the special North Pole mailbox. Inside, more lines wind from the giftwrap station. Shoppers are loading their carts with window candles and serving utensils and stocking stuffers and knitted throws and locally made scented soap. All last-minute items this last weekend before Christmas.

But instead of feeling the Christmas spirit, Harry feels doubt. All he's had with Sadie since Wednesday night are passing glimpses. A nod out the window. A wave from his pickup truck. He's booked at the store; she's booked with Light the Night. Can they make things work? Or did they just get caught up in a moment?

Late afternoon, Harry finally calls Emma to cover the store for him. He heads out for a quick dinner then, stopping at Joel's Bar and Grille to grab a drink and a sandwich. Maybe a complete change of scenery will help clear his head.

∽◯

It doesn't.

Starting with the neon Christmas bells blinking on and off in Joel's front window, it's just more of the same. Happy festivities. Christmas trees on either end of the bar. Silver garland and multicolored twinkly lights looped around the room.

And the couples. Sitting close, toasting one another. Stealing kisses beneath the dangling mistletoe. Wouldn't Harry love to be doing the same with Sadie. But did all these happy couples come together the way he and Sadie did? How can it be that the love of his life is the mysterious woman of the cards he opened for the past eighteen winters?

Sitting at the bar, Harry digs into the turkey wrap he ordered. At least that's done right. Turkey, bacon, shredded Cheddar Jack cheese, and ranch dressing … all of it hits the spot.

"Hey, man," Derek Cooper says when he takes the stool beside Harry. "What's happening, Harry?"

"Oh, Derek." Harry, having just taken another bite of his wrap, wipes a spot of dressing from his jaw. "Just grabbing some chow." He looks past Derek into the noisy bar. "You here with Vera?"

Derek checks his watch. "She's on her way."

"Make an honest woman out of her yet?" Harry asks around a mouthful of his wrap.

"Working on it. We actually got our start here at Joel's.

First kiss," he says while nodding to mistletoe hanging above the bar, "was over there."

"Is that right?"

"Yeah. A few years ago now. Been together ever since." After ordering a beer, he asks Harry, "What about you?"

"What about *me*?"

"Yeah. Nice guy like you, all alone on a Saturday night?"

Harry presses the last of his wrap into his mouth, and washes it down with a long swallow of beer.

"Put it on my tab," Derek tells the bartender when he slides over his draft beer. Derek grabs the glass and turns to Harry then. "So you seeing anyone these days?"

Harry takes another swig of his beer before looking at Derek and telling him about Sadie, and how they kind of did start seeing each other.

"Wait." Derek tips his head. "Sadie, Sadie. She's the one running the Light the Night event?"

"That's her. You met her at the Small Business Christmas Party, right?"

"I did. Nice girl, Harry."

"She is. But, well, some stuff went down, unfortunately. And it's beginning to feel like she's the girl that got away."

"Got away?"

Harry shrugs. "Haven't been able to connect, since … Well, we haven't gotten together in a while."

"You know, Harry." Derek turns his glass on the bar and quiets for a moment. "I'll never forget what you did for me the day I lost Abby."

"Oh, man. It was a tough time for you."

"The worst. And you gave me a coat on the coldest

day of my life." Derek tips his beer to Harry's before taking a long sip. "I'll never forget that. So listen, lay your troubles on me and I'll see what I can do."

Harry does just that. He lays out all his troubles—from the eighteen years of mistaken Christmas cards, to Sadie returning to town, to Harry not telling her about the cards, to their dinner date, to Sadie finding the cards herself and being upset with the discovery.

"But I thought we got past it all, the other night," Harry explains. "I was at her place and we watched some home movies … talked things out. It was good, Derek."

"Wait. Her place. The barn apartment? Where I saw you leaving the other morning when I was plowing snow?"

Harry nods. "You got it. And I thought we had something. But since then, nothing. Eh, a wave here and there. A few words in the store. But you know, the more time that goes by, the more I wonder."

"Don't let her slip away, Harry. Take it from me. You never know how long someone will be here in your life." Derek lifts his glass for another swallow of beer. "You know what you have to do, man."

"That's the problem. I haven't a clue."

"Seriously?"

"Seriously. Got any ideas, guy?"

Derek turns on his swivel stool and faces Harry, straight on. "Listen, Dane. This Sadie, you say she wrote a card to your house every year for the past eighteen winters?"

"She did."

Derek pauses, squinting at Harry for a long second. "Well, my friend. It's your turn now."

⁓

That night, the card rack at SaveRite Grocery Store looks oddly familiar to Harry. There they all are: cards illustrated with gold bells, and crisscrossed candy canes, and peaceful woodland scenes, and jolly Santas, and jaunty snowmen. Each of them a painful reminder of eighteen certain cards he opened over the years.

But. But, but, but. It's those eighteen cards that brought Sadie Welles straight into his life, special delivery it seems now.

Still, Harry's not sure if *this* is the right thing to do. He takes off his wool cap and shoves it in his coat pocket. Buy a card? It seems so insignificant. "*Nah,*" he whispers, then wheels his shopping cart away. He roams a few aisles in the store, which is quiet at this late hour. An older couple's cart is spilling over with food. A young woman hurries past, her arm looped through a basket of apples and fresh bakery rolls. Beneath the garish lighting, Harry picks up a loaf of multigrain bread, a few cans of tomato paste. It's a way to buy some time, dropping these random items into his cart. A way to convince himself that a greeting card will do it. Will bring Sadie back into his life. He sets a container of sea salt in his cart before wheeling it around a woman blocking his way at the cake mixes.

Finally, Harry works his way down the store's rear aisle, past the butters and dairy creamers, until he turns back up the greeting card row. No one else is card shopping at this hour, so the aisle is empty.

Empty of everything except cards. Christmas cards stacked ten high, as far as the eye can see. White poinsettias and loopy red bows and balsam swags. Cardinals on branches; bells tolling; Christmas trees a-glowing. Cards askew. Cards in plastic. Cards sprinkled with glitter. He walks toward those cards again, eyes the rack and pulls out a card with a reindeer illustration, then skims the verse inside. The words—*Joys of the season, friends old and new*—just don't nail it for him. They're not saying what's on his mind. He flips the card over, looks at the others, then puts the reindeer card back and walks away.

But halfway down the aisle, he stops.

Words. Words in a card. *Insignificant?* For eighteen years, all he *had* of Sadie were her words. And they worked. Because all he wants is more words with her, simple as that. Happy words, loving words, caring words. Everyday words. Any words at all.

This might be the only chance he gets—*his* words now, in a card. His one chance to tell Sadie how he really feels. So Harry looks over his shoulder before turning his cart around and heading to the holiday card display once more.

thirty-two

AT DAWN A FEW DAYS later, Sadie arrives at The Green. She zips up her thick fleece jacket. The air already has that Christmas Eve feel to it—wonder and anticipation hover like the early morning mist. Her high school volunteers are also arriving, sipping coffee and cocoa, waiting for direction.

And it doesn't take Sadie long to get them started. The Dane's General Store cargo van backs into its designated space right on schedule. As soon as Harry opens the van's rear doors, the students unload lanterns stacked top to bottom, row upon row.

"Smaller lanterns on the upper bleacher seats," Sadie instructs them, reading from a paper she pulled from her jeans pocket. "Larger on lower. And mix them up on the wall circling the fountain."

"Sadie," Harry says, coming up beside her. "Do you have a minute?"

"Of course. What's up?" she asks, looking back at him. He's got on his wool cap, and a down vest over a thick flannel shirt and jeans. He looks a little tired, too. Or worried. She can't tell which.

"I'd like to stay and help you set up, but the store ..." Harry says as they walk side by side to the wishing fountain area. "Well. We'll be really busy today. You know, being Christmas Eve and all."

"That's okay! You've done so much already," Sadie tells him. "Especially delivering all these lanterns."

Harry looks past her to where the students are setting out hundreds of those lanterns—clustered, circled, scattered. "Do you think you'll have enough?"

Sadie looks, too. "I hope so. Enough to fund a new Christmas tree for The Green, at the very least. I'm told to expect crowds."

"Huh." Harry shakes his head. "To put it mildly. I hear shoppers talking at the store. *Everyone* wants to be a part of this to help get the best tree *ever* back onto The Green."

Then? Nothing. They stand there, looking out at the lanterns being arranged.

"Listen, Sadie," Harry suddenly says, turning her to him.

"Harry," she answers, quietly.

"We'll be closing up the store early. So I'll be back later to see this all light up."

"Okay," she whispers. "I'm glad you'll make it."

"Wouldn't miss it." Harry looks at her, and reaches his hand to touch a wisp of hair escaped from her slouchy knit cap—right as someone calls out her name.

"Miss Welles! Question for you ..."

233

Quickly, Sadie gives Harry's hand a squeeze. "I have to go," she says, then backs up a few steps before turning to assist the waiting volunteers.

Things get even busier on The Green once Harry leaves. Late morning, Derek Cooper arrives with a pickup truck from Cooper Hardware. A pickup whose bed is filled, front to back, with *more* lanterns.

"You don't know this town, Sadie," Derek tells her. "You're going to need every volunteer you can get your hands on—and then some—to light all these."

As she's starting to learn. Once Derek's truck is unloaded early afternoon, families and onlookers and reporters begin arriving. Sadie has just enough time now to rush home, change her clothes and do her hair. And by the time she's back at The Green, the donation tables have wraparound lines. Again and again, she tells folks, "A small donation lights a little lantern. Larger donation, larger lantern."

Everyone is excited to participate. Children drop fistfuls of change on the table. They tell Sadie they emptied their piggy banks to light a lantern. Then there's the young man who secretly reveals that he'll propose to his girlfriend as their lantern is lit. Another couple plans to put a lantern on their fireplace mantel and light it once a year on Christmas Eve, just to remember this night.

As the afternoon goes on, and the twilight sky darkens, soft voices suddenly rise in song. Groups of carolers sing of *joy*, and *silent nights*, and *jingling bells*, and *ships a-sailing*.

Men and women huddle in warm parkas and wool coats. Children's mittened hands hold cups of hot cocoa close. A refreshments tent doles out coffee cake and such. Folks talk, and laugh, and call out Christmas greetings. The bell of the white-steepled chapel tolls in the distance. A horse and carriage circles The Green, the horse's hooves clip-clopping along, its belled harness jingling, too.

But what surprises Sadie most as she leads the lantern-lighting is this: the hush that falls over the crowd. It happens late afternoon when, one by one, little pockets of The Green illuminate.

A flicker here.

A glimmer there.

To the side, silver lanterns hang from tree branches. And on the periphery, hurricane lanterns glow on top of banded wooden barrels. Gradually, lanterns of burnished gold and antique black, tin and wood, shimmer in a circle around the wishing fountain. There are bronze lanterns in more tree branches. Lanterns on shepherds' hooks lining the cobblestone walkway.

All around Sadie, The Green has gone quiet. Lantern lights flicker on, twinkle, sparkle like winter fireflies rising to the sky.

But the crowd especially delights in the evening's grand finale. Sadie hears murmurs and random whistles. Applause grows. Her high school volunteers had the perfect idea. They filled the portable bleachers with lanterns arranged in the shape of a tall Christmas tree. Little by little, those lanterns—some candle, some battery-operated—illuminate the lantern-tree. When they're all lit, and that topmost lantern is flickering close to the dark sky, it happens.

It's even more beautiful than Sadie had imagined all those weeks ago when she thought up this event. Suddenly, light takes over the dark night. Lantern light wavers golden. Hundreds and hundreds of small flames shine and glimmer, casting a misty hue over The Green.

❦

Harry's not sure he's ever seen a more enchanted sight. In the dark solemnity of Christmas Eve, all of Addison is on the town green. Families and couples—young and old, bundled in coats and hats—watch in hushed silence. The lantern illumination casts some sort of holiday spell on each and every onlooker. Heads are tipped up. Folks point to their favorite lantern. People wipe tears from their cheeks. Over on the side, he notices Lorrie and Allan and gives a wave. Other couples hold each other close. Children are hoisted on fathers' shoulders to take in the sight.

Harry takes it in, too. But only for a few moments. Then he searches the crowd for Sadie. Once he spots her near the town dignitaries about to thank everyone for making Light the Night happen, he moves a little closer. Sadie, of course, is also thanked for her innovation and generosity of spirit in putting this most special evening together.

And when the talks are done, and families wander off—either to church services or Christmas Eve dinners in grand old homes—Harry walks to Sadie standing near the podium.

"There you are!" she softly exclaims.

Harry stops beside her, puts an arm around her waist and talks close. "It all looks so beautiful," he says. "You did an amazing job here."

"Oh, Harry." Sadie turns to him, then looks at the lanterns against the dark night. "It was a labor of love. Do you see what lightness in the night brings to people?"

"People here?"

"Yes. There's peace. And wonder. Hope. Hope, too."

Harry steps back and hesitates. He looks from the lanterns to Sadie. She'd changed for the event. Her long blonde hair falls in loose waves now. She wears a thick, soft gray scarf wrapped up around her neck, the scarf tucked into a half-zipped moto jacket over dark velvet pants and ankle boots.

"Harry?" she asks. "You're quiet. Is everything okay?"

Well, he's about to find out. Because during the past few days, Harry wasn't always sure this moment would arrive. "Walk with me, Sadie?" he asks, holding out his gloved hand.

She gives a small smile, puts her hand in his, and together they circle the lantern-lit green. They don't say much as a few familiar faces wish Harry a merry Christmas. Some of Sadie's coworkers are there, too. They give her a hug while thanking her for this magical Christmas Eve.

But finally, there is only Sadie and himself, and the lingering stragglers taking in the sight of glimmering candlelight.

"Sadie." Harry looks at Sadie beside him. "We've both been so busy these past few days, I'm glad we finally have a chance to talk."

"Me too, Harry."

"The thing is, I've had something on my mind." Still holding her mittened hand, Harry talks while they walk in the lanterns' glow around the wishing fountain. "The other day. When we watched the home movies, and spent the night together, it was really nice. And I want to be sure."

"Sure of what?"

"Of us." Harry takes a long breath. "Can you really forgive me for never returning your cards all those years? For never sending you a note, or finding Lorrie and Allan." He pauses, and Sadie says nothing. "Never writing *Return to Sender* on the envelopes."

"Forgive you?" Sadie asks while their walk slows. "I *thank* you."

"What?" Harry can't believe the words he's hearing. "Thank me?"

"Yes. For coming into my life the way you did."

He looks at her then. Really looks at her. Her eyes are moist; her smile, genuine. "Sadie. I feel like I've *known* you all my life."

"In a way, you have."

Harry takes her hand again and leads her to a snow-dusted bench. He sweeps off the snow and sits beside her there. From the low branches of nearby trees, lanterns dangle, casting wavering golden light on them. Before he says anything else, Harry reaches an arm around Sadie's shoulders and lightly kisses the top of her head. When he sits back, she leans into him, pressing close.

"I'll never tire of this sight," she softly says, looking out at the lantern-strung branches, at the glimmering lantern-lit stone wall circling the wishing fountain.

"Sadie," Harry begins then. Yes, begins. Because right now, he hopes this moment is the start of something more. "For the past eighteen winters, you sent your card. Your words." He pauses, swallowing some emotion that's taken hold. "Sent your heart ... right into my home."

"I did," she tells him. Tells him with no regret, no remorse. With only gentleness.

"I don't have eighteen cards for you, Sadie." He reaches inside his coat to the interior pocket. "I just have one."

Sadie looks at him when he holds out the envelope. Wordlessly, she takes it. After tugging off her mittens, she lightly traces the edge of the envelope, then flips it from one side to the other.

"Open it," he barely whispers.

When she does, carefully, and pulls out the card, he looks at the image on it. Sees it the way she might. In the illustration, branches of a snow-laden pine tree brush against a paned country window. The card depicts a winter's night—snow gathering in the corners of the window's shadowy panes, a lit candle nestled in greens on the windowsill. The candlelight throws a soft glow on the darkness of the room inside. Something about the card said Addison to Harry. And home. And spoke of love within that home. Love and longing. He wonders now if Sadie sees the same things.

Sitting with him on the bench, Sadie opens the card and reads the verse inside. But when she stops and looks to Harry, he knows. He knows it's not the card's verse that makes her look at him. Makes her touch his face, his hair. Makes her fight back tears.

No, it's his words. His personal words written beneath the verse. His simple words offered after reading *her* penned words for the past eighteen winters.

But right now, he's at a loss for words. Instead, he turns up his hands and only hopes.

So Sadie? Well, she looks at his card again, and this time reads aloud the note he'd written across the bottom. Her voice is soft, and catches with emotion. "*Spend this eighteenth winter with me?*"

Time seems to stop then. Each silent second is an eternity as Sadie drags her finger across Harry's words, then looks up at him on this cold Christmas Eve.

"And the next winter?" she asks.

When he realizes what she's saying—that she's not turning him down—he briefly closes his eyes, then looks at her and only nods, slowly.

"And the next, after that?" she whispers.

Harry nods again. Nods, then takes her face in his hands and kisses her, right there on the snowy green. Lantern light glimmers in the tree branches above them; a wintry breeze blows. "Sadie," he says. "I have to tell you something."

"What is it, Harry?" she asks.

"For the past eighteen winters, I've been falling in love with you." He hesitates when Sadie reaches up and brushes her fingers across his jaw. "And I don't want to spend another winter without you," he tells her.

With lanterns flickering like stars around them, glowing golden against the dark December sky, Sadie tells him that she doesn't either. And when he hears her murmured words after another kiss, tender words whispered close, Harry looks briefly at that night sky. There's no moon tonight, so the sky is black. But tiny pinpricks of starlight dot it, far, far above. Those stars, scattered across the darkness, they seem to flicker like the lanterns surrounding him. In the night, hopeful, and promising, all at once.

ENJOY MORE OF
THE WINTER NOVELS

1) Snowflakes and Coffee Cakes

2) Snow Deer and Cocoa Cheer

3) Cardinal Cabin

4) First Flurries

5) Eighteen Winters

6) Winter House

— And more Winter Novels —

FROM NEW YORK TIMES BESTSELLING AUTHOR
JOANNE DEMAIO

Also by Joanne DeMaio

For a complete list of books by *New York Times* bestselling author Joanne DeMaio, visit:

Joannedemaio.com

About the Author

JOANNE DEMAIO is a *New York Times* and *USA Today* bestselling author of contemporary fiction. She enjoys writing about friendship, family, love and choices, while setting her stories in New England towns or by the sea. Joanne lives with her family in Connecticut and is currently at work on her next novel.

For a complete list of books and for news on upcoming releases, please visit Joanne's website. She also enjoys hearing from readers on Facebook.

Author Website:
Joannedemaio.com

Facebook:
Facebook.com/JoanneDeMaioAuthor